Confessions of a Coyote

One Printers Way
Altona, MB R0G 0B0
Canada

www.friesenpress.com

First Edition — 2022

ISBN
978-1-03-915375-2 (Hardcover)
978-1-03-915374-5 (Paperback)
978-1-03-915376-9 (eBook)

1. FICTION, INDIGENOUS

Distributed to the trade by The Ingram Book Company

Confessions of a Coyote

As told by Stella Coyote

NANCY LAFLEUR

THE MAKING OF STELLA COYOTE

DISCLAIMER

This book is gonna kill you no matter how you look at it. Either my poor grammar and spelling will get you, or my stories and crazy confessions. I am not much of a writer, and I ain't got much of an education, so if you see mistakes in this book, just know that I'm not aiming to please the grammar police. I am writing 'cause that is all I got to do right now. I would like to add that this book is not for you young ones. It might not be even for those who don't like the swear words and a little dirty talk too. Don't say I didn't warn you. Read at your own risk. I hope you enjoy my story.

Stella Coyote

HEY, IT'S ME, STELLA

I am not sure how this will go, but best I can do is give it a try, right? This book thing, I mean. Heck, I don't know nothing about writing, but what the hell, I will give it a shot anyways. Shit, I've done crazy things in my life, so maybe sharing some of these stories might be a good thing. I don't know what to say about my life except that crazy shit just seems to follow me, and it seemed like I had no real control of stuff, and so I just went with the flow. Maybe that's how life is for most folks—not having any real control, so most just do what they can to survive. Thing is, survival is my life story and so I guess I will share some parts with you all. Maybe writing is something to look forward to, and the cool part is, I can share whatever I want. Some might believe me, and some won't, but that's okay 'cause this is my story. and maybe it's time I shared a thing or two. And to be honest, I don't know if I will even stick around here long enough to finish this book once I start it, but I think I will give it an honest try anyways. Bouncing and moving has been the story of my life—living from one moment to the next, just day to day. No worries about what tomorrow might bring. Maybe that's what makes a good story. I don't know. All I know is I was told to maybe write my stories 'cause some of the things I done and seen might make for some good reading, and maybe even a few good laughs. That's me. Good time Stella. No worries in the world 'cause I have no time for bullshit. Okay, I will admit that at times I've been scared, but shit, who hasn't been, and anyone who says they have never been scared is a liar. But I don't live in fear. I can't. Worry and fear will kill you, and no matter what, I still kind of like living. My life is a moving story, kind of like a river. So, just giving you all a fair warning, you get what you get with me. Sometimes I swear, so I am warning you. If you can't handle the real Coyote, then no use wasting your time reading. **This is my story, and I guess it starts here.**

I GOT LOTS TO TELL YA

My life has been a crazy place, and there were times, I will admit, that I wasn't sure where I was going to end up. I best sum it up like a flowing river; some spots have been rough, but one thing I learned about rivers is once you get through the rough spots, there is usually something calm waiting on the other end. My life has been much like that: craziness then calm, craziness then calm. In all honesty, this is the longest calm I've had in a long time, and I am not sure what to think. After all, you can't just take an animal from the wild and think the bugger is going to get all cute and calm in one day. Shit don't work that way. **I've been just surviving this crazy thing they call life and winging it as I go.** In the end, we will all have the same ending and end up in the same place, so best thing for me is to do what I can now, and not get worked up over shit I can't control. There is too much hate in this world. Truth is, my life has been an interesting place to be, and getting older kind of has me thinking back to how things were, how things got to the way they went, and maybe has me even thinking and wondering on why I fought to survive this life. Thing is, I tried my best to bury my past long ago. Wasn't a good place to be so I done my best to erase them memories. There is lots of pain down in my past. I don't want to live there and there was no way that shit was going to drag me down. The way I see it, I can live in misery and spend my days feeling sorry for myself, or I can make the best of things. And I guess I was always a bit of a dreamer and wanted just a little happiness, maybe some laughter along the way. It's sad when I see people get stuck in that hole of loneliness. It's an awful place to be and it seems that once a person falls into that shit hole of pain, it is hard to drag themselves out again. I feel for them, you know. Maybe I seen enough of it to try harder. Maybe that is why I just move like a river too. Just maybe, I am running from that shit that might destroy me. I sure as hell don't want that. Did all kinds of things to stay away from everything that happened so long ago. That stuff seems so far away, but sometimes them memories just sneak back up on me. I tell myself, "Stella, not much you can do about those things now, so why cry over spilled tea, right?" So, I decided a long time ago that I would make other memories to try to cover them bad ones. **I made a rule long ago to live in the now! In the today!**

I lost contact with my family a long time ago, so I decided not to get so hung up on missing them. Well, at least that is what I kept telling myself anyways. Thing is, them memories of what happened—well, they don't really go away. Yeah, I tried to run from them, even told myself that the past is the past. And sure, it is that—the past—but now and again them bitchin' memories just come creeping up. I've been to places, and I met lots of people; along the way they became my family for the time being. So, with that being said, I have family everywhere I go. I have sisters, brothers, aunties, and uncles, and of course, cousins all over the countryside. Never got married either, so the title "husband" never made my list of family members. Yes, I borrowed a few men along the way. Yeah, yeah, I know, not cool, but this is my reality, my story. Another thing I never had was kids, at least none of my own. Not really sure how that happened, but I am thinking that I probably couldn't have none. Well, I had a few kids call me mommy or auntie but never had none to really call my own. Maybe that was a good thing too. I mean, this one time, my friend asked me to babysit her plants, and they all died on me. I think it would have been scary to have kids; not sure how well I could have taken care of a kid. I just survive to look after myself.

I figure the writing of my book is my chance to reflect on all my adventures, share a few stories, and maybe confess to stuff that's been bugging me a little. I've seen some hard times, some good times, fun times, loving times, and hating times throughout this life, and sitting back now and thinking, I sometimes wonder how I survived everything that came my way. It was a rough start, my life, and even thinking back to them days, I am surprised I am still alive. I did things that could have had me in big trouble, but somehow everything worked out, and here I am.

My biggest problem right now is getting started. I ain't never written a book before. Thing is, never thought I would. But opportunity has me time, and it's paid time, so that's a pretty good deal for me. So, why not? I remember back in my school days, I used to love to write. Heck, it was all we did. My friends and I would write letters all day long in class as to not piss off the teachers. They were mean back then. The teachers. Seemed it didn't matter where I lived; most teachers were just miserable people. There were a few nice ones, but it seemed I never got to be in their classrooms. I always seemed to end up with them grumpy ones. Maybe that is one reason I never went back to school to finish. Bad memories just steered me clear from school. It's crazy when I think about it now—the power teachers have on kids. Can make them or break them. I don't think I really had a chance from the get-go. Most teachers didn't seem to warm up to me. I guess I was just one of them kids that once labelled with something, that label was bound to follow me anywhere I went. I mean, I was a foster kid. A kid that belonged to the system. We must have been a "kind," if you know what I mean. I get pissy when I think about it now. Them fucking teachers that treated us like garbage just 'cause we didn't come from one of them "stable homes" as they called them. They just thought us foster kids were trouble. The sad part is, at some point, trouble is what got us into care, just not our trouble. I met lots of foster kids in my travels, and the sad part is, none of us asked to be foster kids, and none of us would choose that life if given the option. The shit part is, somewhere down the road, we end up in care 'cause there is no one else around to look after us. As a grown person, thinking back to all my stuff, I guess it does make me wonder why I didn't have a fair shot in life. I didn't come from one of them families with the mom and dad, the car, the house, and the little brothers and sisters that just bugged the shitoutta you, but you loved them anyways! Never had that. Wish I did, but apparently, that wasn't in the "plan." You know, the "plan." **Life's plan!** I heard somewhere that everyone has one that was given to them at birth or something. I don't know. I hear people talk sometimes, and sometimes I do listen. This is how I ended up learning about, the "plan." Apparently, everyone comes born with a blueprint, and so whatever is happening to a person is supposed to happen that way. So, yeah, I guess I am a bit bitter. Like, how the hell does that happen anyways? Is there like a deck of cards, and whatever "plan" you get from the deck, you're stuck with? Or does it depend on a person's skin colour, 'cause from where I am standing, us brown skins kind of got the raw end of the deck. But I'm not going to harp on that shit right now; life is life. I got given what I was given. I know stuff happens, but at any given moment, someone somewhere could have made a better choice as to not set the course for someone else. I think maybe this is the part where I am supposed to get angry at my dad for setting the stage for how my life became. But like I said before, I'm not going to get hung up on that shit. It lives in the past. **My dad, my mom, my family—gone with it!**

Where has this old Coyote been, and where will it all end? I have so many questions, so much time to think about. As I sit here and stare at this computer screen, so many memories come flooding through, and not all of them are complete. I remember moments of my childhood, a few good stories, some not-so-good ones, and some are foggy. My memories start in Birch Creek, Saskatchewan. I grew up there as a kid for the first years of my life. From Birch Creek, I have been all over Canada, so my stories and my memories are all over the land. I have visited Toronto, Vancouver, and everywhere in between. I even ended up in Yellow Knife one time. I don't carry much in my travels. My memories come when I hear a song or see a map of a place I've been. Don't really collect that souvenir stuff, and even if I did, I would have lost everything by now anyways.

I just learned to use a computer recently. Never really had time to learn much when I was living to survive, but about a year ago, my luck turned, and I landed this job, and it led me to having a computer to use, to learn on. I work for the Evans family. Old Mr. Evans was in some sort of accident. I don't know, they didn't give me much details, and it's none of my business to ask. But anyhow, he fell into a coma, and been in one for over a year. At first, they kept him in the hospital, but the wife wanted him at home here, so they decided to hire someone to look after him while she run their business. I haven't known the Evans family for that long, but for some crazy reason, they took a liking to me, and I really liked them too. They are nice people, and for some reason, I trust them. They weren't like them creepy couples I would run into from time to time, trying to hire me to do weird sex things with them. Honestly, though. Well, it was just this one time when this one couple wanted me to dress up like a pirate for their fantasy or something. But anyways, I am getting off track, so back to my story.

It's kind of funny how this all started, but I was working at a Pet Shop, you know, them places they sell dogs and other animals. I was in this small city called Elbow Summit, close to Regina. I had come here after leaving Vancouver to be closer to home, whatever the hell that meant, but I had a connection for a job here, so I took it. Anyway, I was the night cleaner at this pet shop but would sometimes go in during store hours so I could just visit the dogs. I felt sorry for them little guys, being boxed in them cages. I couldn't imagine what was going on in their minds, but I figured they got lonesome. Anyways, I was visiting the dogs one day and carrying one when this couple come in. The lady—she likes the dog I am carrying, but each time she try to pick him up, the dog starts barking at her. He just did not like her for some reason. Well, she gets her shit all up in a knot and starts complaining like there is some kind of magic to having a dog warm up to you, so I tell her to sit down. She sits for a bit, and I tell her to close her eyes and imagine herself walking the dog. And to be clear, I am making the shit up as I go, pretending I am some kind of dog whisperer and stuff. But anyway, she's sitting there closing her eyes, and I tell her that I am going to place the dog gently on her lap, and to keep her eyes closed. She listens to me. I tell her to relax, and to slow her breathing. I wait a few minutes like I know what I'm doing, then I put the dog on her lap. Her husband is looking at me like I am crazy. I tell her to gently place her hand on the dog and pet gently. The dog is calm. Her eyes are still closed. She pets the dog gently, and the dog just sits there enjoying the good petting. I tell her to open her eyes slowly, but to not look at the dog. She does this. I tell her to keep petting the dog. Pretty soon her and the dog—well, they connect. The husband, he tells me I am good and asks what I do there. I tell him I am the janitor. He tells me he likes me and asks how many hours I work in a day. I tell him I work about four hours a day, mostly in the evenings, but I like to come in and visit the pets. He tells me he owns the hardware shop just up the road and needs someone to stock shelves and tidy up the place. He then asks if I am looking for extra work, and of course I tell him, "Yeah." He tells me I can work first thing in the morning, which I accept. I am not much of a morning person, but I tell him I could use the extra cash. He hires me right there on the spot. It was like winning a scratchy that day. This was how I met the Evans family. I had a good thing going, working at Evans Hardware in the mornings, then the pet shop after closing hours. It was like things were actually going my way for a change.

Anyway, to make a long story short, one day I show up the Evans Hardware store, and the "closed" sign is still on. I know something is wrong, and so I start asking around town if anyone knew where the Evans might be. No one seemed to know a thing, until Mrs. Evans, Judy, shows up at the pet store later that day and tell me that there was an accident the night before, and Mr. Evans was not in good shape. She tells me they are closing the store for a few days and that she would keep me posted. I didn't ask questions, 'cause I knew it wasn't my place, but I will admit I was worried about the old man. He had been real good to me and all. Even gave me advanced money when I was real broke. Anyways, Judy doesn't come back to the pet shop for a few weeks, and I don't go snooping around but was worried about my other paycheck too. One day, she walks in and tells me that Mr. Evans was alive but still in a coma from his accident. She tells me that the store would be closed until they knew more. I tell her I understand and would be there when they needed me back. About a month later, she walks in again, but this time, she asks me if I could be a caregiver to Mr. Evans while she works the store. She explains that they can't keep the store closed much longer and really needed my help. She tells me she wants the old man at home, and that a nurse would help with the care, but in between, she wants someone there for him for when he wakes up. At first, I wasn't sure what she meant by that, but then she explained that Mr. Evans is in a coma, and that she had made preparations to have him moved to her home where he would get care from a nurse, and from a caregiver. She tells me that I would have to quit my job at the pet shop, but she would pay real good for caring for Mr. Evans. I think about her offer for a few minutes and tell her she's got herself a deal.

The first few weeks were real boring, sitting here and staring at Mr. Evans, waiting for him to wake up. He just looks like he's sleeping. The nurse comes in a few times a day to change his feeding tube, take some tests, and some other stuff that I don't stick around to watch. The doctor comes by once a day just to make sure everything is good. I figure this is what the rich do—pay people like me to care for them. I'm not complaining or anything, but I had never seen anything like this where people set up a hospital in their own home. Well, maybe it happens, but I just never knew people like this before. Anyways, the nurse, she teaches me what to look for and how to turn him every few hours so he doesn't get sore laying in the same position. So, in between turns and checking things, there was not much else to do, so I explained to Judy that I need something to do to pass the time. That was when she suggested I write a book about my life. She and I would sit for tea sometimes, and I would tell her stories. I think I may have even told her that I used to like to write at some point in my life, so I guess that was why she told me to start writing again. I tell her that I haven't written for years, and probably forgot how to. She tells me that writing is like riding a bike—that once you learn, you don't forget. When she said that, I just chuckled. Not at her, but thinking about my ol' buddy Kathy, who they use to call Bicycle. Anyway, I don't think that rule applies to her on the not forgetting part, 'cause I think anyone who had a ride with her wanted to forget real quick. And it wasn't 'cause Kathy was ugly or anything; she just had a big mouth and would share the stories about her victim and their wiener size and all. Kathy was crazy like that. I wonder, what ever happened to her? My guess is, she too got old and rusty. But anyways, Mrs. Evan, she tells me that I am a good storyteller, and that people like to read good stories like mine. She tells me I can use her computer to write, and so I explain I don't know how to use a computer. She tells me not to worry, that she'd show me how to use it. She gives me some quick lessons that day, and so I decide writing was better than just sitting and staring at Mr. Evans all day. Truth is, using the computer wasn't really that hard, and writing my stories was not that hard either. So, this is how this adventure of writing really started for me. **I got lots to tell ya.**

THE EARLY YEARS

I guess the best place to start is from the beginning. I was born with the legal name Stella Bella Coyote, (pronounced Ki-yo-teee). I was born on May 10th, 1962. I was born in Prince Albert, Saskatchewan to Marie and John Coyote. The Coyote family was a small one, and I don't really remember too many others having the same last name. My father was John Coyote, and he was married to my mother, Marie Coyote. There were five of us in my family. I had three brothers and a sister. We all got separated at a young age, but I still remember them. I am the oldest of the Coyote bunch. My brothers were Frank, Hank, and Earl. My sister, her name was Connie. My sister Connie Coyote was the middle child. Our birth order was me, Stella Coyote, then my brother Frank Coyote, then Connie Coyote, Hank Coyote, and last was our baby brother who was born with 11 fingers, Earl Coyote.

I remember we lived in a small Reserve called Birch Creek just northwest of Prince Albert, Saskatchewan. A Reserve is those pieces of land they put the Indians on after treaties were signed. In all my travels to Reserves, it looked like us Indians got a bad deal 'cause all the good land was taken and we were left with whatever the government couldn't make money from. Anyways, I remember the ride to Prince Albert was not a long one, but it wasn't too often we would go either. My dad worked for a local farmer and so he would stay home during the winter months and drink his life away. My mom worked at the school as the janitor and so she brought in steady money. I remember lots of farmland and fields, and houses spread apart from one another. I also remember this long lake. I remember when we were kids, mom and dad would sometimes drive us to the lake, and I would go swimming. We were pretty young, but I still remember how they would pack up some food for a picnic. We would spend the day there. The kids would swim, and mom and dad would hang back by the trees and drink. It wasn't often that dad did not drink during those times. Mom didn't always drink with him, but I think she just got tired of seeing his drinking and so joining him was a better choice in her mind. Like I said before, I'm still not convinced this was all part of the 'plan' 'cause in the end, that drinking gone and ruined everything for us. Anyways, we were not that old when the cops come knocking on our door. I was home babysitting. I think I was about nine years old. My mom and dad had gone to Prince Albert to grocery shop. I knew they would be out drinking too. I hated it when they would come home drunk and crazy. Sometimes they would be laughing and loving each other, acting like they had just met at the bar, and sometimes they would be fighting, bringing up the past and all. It was evening already, and they still hadn't come home. But somehow, I didn't think nothing of it. I was used to them leaving and staying late. Anyways, this one particular night, it was summer, and my dad must have got paid 'cause he gave us each five dollars before they left. We were at home, the five of us. The boys were in their bedroom playing, and me and Connie were in the living room watching TV. There was a knock at our door, which was kind of weird 'cause mostly, people would just walk in. It was safe to keep your door unlocked in them days. Anyways, I don't open the door, figuring someone would just walk through the door like they usually do. Then, there was another knock, then another. I remember being scared 'cause no one knocked like that before, so I just walk quietly to the door, and pressed my ear up against it. I'm not sure what I was thinking doing that, but for some reason it seemed to make sense. I remember putting my finger to my lips and shushing my siblings who by now had made their way to the door because of the knocking noise. I whisper for them to be quiet. The funny thing is, the door was not even locked 'cause like I says before, no one ever locked their doors back then.

I listen at the door, then I hear a voice on the other side saying, "This is the Police."

I was really scared then, thinking they came to get us for being home alone. I open the door for the cop to come in. He asks who is looking after us, and I tell him that my mom and dad are just next door. He tells me he knows I am lying to him. I ask him how he know that, and he asks again if there are any adults around. I finally tell him that I am babysitting and so he asks if I have grandparents. I tell him there is nobody. He leaves back to his car, tells me to stay put, and to gather my brothers and sister. He comes back again, but this time comes straight into the house. I was nine years old. I am not sure, but I think my brother Frank was about eight. Connie would have been six, Hank, I am guessing, was five, and baby Earl would have been four. I think that's right 'cause I remember my mom always being pregnant, and it just seemed like us kids were a staircase.

I do what the cop says to do and gather the boys and my sister. We sit in the living room, waiting for the cop to get back, and I remember how quiet we all became not knowing what was happening. I just thought they came to get us 'cause we got left alone—that's all. That would be the last night I see them all. I still remember that look on their faces when the lady with the black jacket came and took us away. I know now that it was Social Services. I didn't back then. My mom and dad, they got killed that night in a car accident. I learned later by one of my social workers that my dad was driving drunk. That was a bad night. Saddest part was never seeing my brothers and sister again, never seeing my mom and dad again.

That night. I haven't thought about that night in a long, long time. I was the oldest; it was supposed to be my job to care for the others, but that never happened. I never got the chance. No one wanted all five of us kids, so we got separated. I was placed in home in Regina. A place so far away from Birch Creek. I never knew where the others went. This happened in the early '70s. I was just a fucking kid, man. I had no choice in all this shit. Great plan someone had for me! Right?

My first home was a good home, and I got along with the folks well. I went to school, did my chores, and got a little allowance at the end of the week. It was hard those first few months, and I cried a lot. I wanted to see my sister and my brothers, but it never happened. I put my mind into writing, and when I got my allowance, I would buy myself some fancy paper. Sometimes I would draw pictures. I would draw places I wanted to visit one day. Places I had seen in magazines. I remember seeing this beautiful place with a white sand beach in a National Geographic magazine. The water was clear blue, and I could see the seashells laying on the bottom of the sand waters. I would dream of that place when things got rough. I would rip pages out of those magazines and slip them in my notebooks. When I got lonesome, I would take the pictures out and dream. Other times I would write. I don't remember much of what I wrote, but I just remember writing stuff in my notebooks. I stayed at my first home for three years. I didn't understand why I had to leave, but I was told that the home only allowed children to stay for a certain amount of time, and I had used up mine. They were pretty good years too. I hated having to leave. I was twelve when I left, and it seems that this was when my life made its turn.

My next home was a nightmare. This place was in nearby Moose Jaw. There were four other kids there. We were all foster kids. There were two boys and two girls, and with me there was three girls in total. All of us girls shared a room, and sharing a room meant we all had to sleep in one bed. I hated it. The girls I remember were named Janey and Debra. They were sisters. I learned to smoke my first cigarette from Debra. I haven't quit smoking since. The boys stayed in the room across the hall from us. I didn't like them much. They were always up to something bad, and although I tried to stay out of that crap, it somehow seemed to find me. The boys, Bruce and Harty (I don't think that was his name),smoked marijuana. I remember this one night I was just coming home from visiting my friend Mona from across the street. I remember walking across the road and the wind picking up. The house we lived in had a bush fence, and I could hear laughing from around the other side, so I get scared and turn to cross the road. Anyway, before I could cross, Harty jumps out and scares the shit out of me, and I scream. The scream is loud enough to bring our foster mom to the front door; she opens it and catches the boys smoking pot. She yells at all of us to get the hell into the house, and as we're walking in, I tell her I had nothing to do with the smoking. Grumpy old bitch doesn't believe me, and so I tell her to just fuck off.

Had never really sworn at anyone before, but I will admit it felt pretty good. She tells us to get to bed and that she would call our workers the next day to come remove us. I didn't give her the opportunity. That night when the crooked-nosed witch went to bed, I grabbed my bag, put some clothes and food in it, and walked out the front door. So, here I was, twelve years old, on the run to God only knows where. The only real place I know to go was the school yard 'cause I knew it had a few sheds out back. It was scary, but as scary as it was, I found my way to the school and managed to get into one of the sheds and slept in it. I think this is when my knack to survive really kicked in. I had made up my mind to leave that night, and there was no one in the world who was going to stop me. I learned to be tough that night, and I learned that there was no one I could trust to look out for me. I just had myself, and there was no way in bloody hell I would let them bastards take me down. This tough thinking got me through the night, and now when I think back to that time, that tough thinking got me through lots of tough times. Anyways, once I told myself that I would be ok, I wasn't as scared anymore. I knew I just had to do things to help keep me safe, and so that was what I did. I found a stick lying beside the door of the shed, so I picked it up and took it in the shed with me. I would be my weapon if I needed something. Once I got into the shed, I found some boards lying around, so I took a few and jammed them up against the door. I knew if someone was trying to come in, they would have their work cut out for them. Next, I found a few plywood sheets, so I made myself a makeshift bed, covering myself with the jacket I walked out with and using my backpack as a pillow. I slept that night without a worry in the world, telling myself that I would always be tougher than what the world was going to throw at me. At that time, I wasn't sure what the 'plan' was for me, but my best guess was that life was not going to get easy for this Coyote. I woke the next morning with the sun shining through a hole in the ceiling, and to voices talking outside. I took my time getting up, afraid to move, afraid they would hear me. I sat up and tried to work the crimps out of my back from sleeping on the boards.

My escape didn't last too long. The voices outside were the cops. They caught me that morning and hauled me back to my foster home. I pleaded for them to take me to my worker, but they didn't listen. Instead, they drove me back to the witch's house. As we were driving back, I started thinking back to that time my buddy and I ran away from school at Birch Creek. We were about eight years old. Anyway, we were outside playing when my buddy says, "Let's run away from school."

I don't even answer, and she bolts to the fence. I chase her, not really knowing where we are going, and all I see is Mr. Oliver running behind us, yelling for us to get back. We run through Mrs. Bird's fence and go hide in her shed. We stay in there, quiet, waiting for Mr. Oliver to find us, but he doesn't. We spent the rest of the day playing cat and mouse with him. It was the best day ever, until we got home. Our moms were pretty mad at us. I was grounded, but it didn't last too long. My mom and dad started drinking a few nights later and forgot I was grounded. That's how it was. So, I guess in a sense, I was already practicing to be a runner back then.

Anyway, we got back to the foster home in time to meet up with the social workers. They meet me at the car, and they tell me that I have to go with them. I am okay with it, as long as I didn't have to stay in the one I just ran from. I figured it couldn't get any worse, but it did. My next foster home was in a mostly white little-shit-farm-town in Manitoba. Holy shit, I didn't realize how brown I really was until I got there. The family I stayed with, well, they meant well, but it just seemed like they always felt sorry for me. Don't get me wrong, I liked the attention at first, but after a while, even I was starting to feel sorry for myself.

The kids at school were horrible people. I think they taught me to hate white people more. They were a good lesson about the things I would never get in life. Like a nice home, a family, and all the things these families did together. They taught me to have no expectations, that way, I could never get disappointed. But they also taught me to hate the colour of my skin and theirs.

They reminded me each and every day that I was different, and after a while, I even accepted that maybe there was a natural order in the human race. Just like the food chain I had learned about in school. Us brown skins—well, we were the bacteria or the rot from the animals after they died, feeding the plants. I really started to believe that about myself. I really felt that I was less than the white kids, and they did a great job of treating me like I was less human than they were. Of course, when I got older, I seen the wrong side of that whiteness and knew they were no cookie cutter Martha Stewart types. I became very untrusting of them—the white kids and their parents. And soon, I learnt to sort them bastards out. There were the ones that just plain-out hated us brown skins, and they weren't shy about it either. They treated us like we were dumb. They treated us like we weren't even human, like we were nothing but drunks and thieves. Those hatful kids. They talked badly about us browns and sometimes I would overhear them. Some of them were cruel enough to even say shit to my face, or say stuff and pretend I wasn't even there, like I was invisible. We were outnumbered in that school, us brown skins, so no one cared if we got mad. At first, I tried to argue back, but I learned real fast that there were battles I would not win. It fueled my hatred and my willingness to fight, but not in a good way. Later in life, I mostly fought with my hands, and the vulgarity that spewed out of my mouth. I had to let everyone know that I was tougher than the shit they were throwing my way.

Then there was them white folks that acted like God put them on earth to save us poor brown skins, kind of like the foster parents I was with. I mean, they were okay and all, but it just seemed they didn't trust us enough to look after ourselves or even do things for ourselves. They were the ones that should have worn those big light up signs that read, "Save a brown skin, go to heaven," or something like that. I met many on my travels, and the thing was, I had become a survivor, and I learned quick to take what I could take before it got taken from me.

Then lastly, of course, I just have to mention those that belonged to the "Wannabe Tribe." I laughed when I was told the meaning of this. They just wanna be Indian without the bad things. I am sure it was just some crazy fad they was going through. And did they really even know what being Indian really was about? I honestly don't think any of them would have traded their white skin and place in society to really become one of us. Don't get me wrong, I love the skin that was given to me, but we had it tough with how we get treated in schools and other places. Heck, even if we are walking around shopping in stores, they think we going to steal right from under them. It is harder to get jobs and rent places on the count of our skin colour. The funny thing about that whole thing is, there are bigger thieves stealing way bigger things than an Indian stealing a t-shirt. They just don't think of them other things 'cause they act like it's all different. Some people just watched too much darn TV and thought Pocahontas was some romance. If only they knew the truth. Truth was, Pocahontas was one of our first missing and murdered Indian women. How's that for the history books? That shit started right from the start. My guess is, fucking Columbus probably raped more women than any of us will ever know. Don't get me wrong, I wouldn't trade my brown skin for any colour in this whole wide world, but it was tough living in a world where everything was taken from us and we was the ones looked down on like thieves. That shit is just ass backwards in my books.

The nice thing was I never really seen the Evans family in any other these categories. I just seen them as my fella humans. That's all. I used to believe there were only certain types of people that fell into my categories, but until I met the Evans family, wel,l I guess they showed me different. They were just good people.

Anyway, the kids at my new school that I am talking about were mean. They teased me, calling me "Indian." Then they would start clapping on those big white mouths and start making them noises. You know the ones. The kind people make to try to sound, "Indian." I remember this one boy, Brian. Anyway, he was the worst of them bunch. Well, one day I just lose my cool and chase him into the park. I forget I have my skipping rope in my hand. He runs towards a path in the park that separates the park and a few houses. Anyways, I catch that little bastard in the trail and tie him up to a tree with my skipping rope. I tell that little shit that if he ever messed with me again, I would scalp that blonde hair off his head. I was serious. He knew it. He musta seen the rage when I said, "I have had enough of your shit, and now you just really pissed me off!"

The kid almost shit himself, crying like he was going to die. I mean, I was crazy in my day, but I would never kill a person. Mind you, if something would have happened to him, no judge or jury would have taken my side. After all, I was just a brown-skinned kid in foster care. Anyways, he begged me to let him go and so I left him there tied up to the tree. I knew eventually someone would come along and save his white ass. He never told anyone, and he never teased me again. Brain showed me exactly what I had to do to deal with the idiots of the world if they got in my way. Again, another learned lesson on survival.

I stayed at the foster home in Manitoba until I was fifteen, and I managed to finish grade ten. After that, I left on my own free will. I hitchhiked back to Regina. It was the closest city that had familiarity and so I thought it was as good as place as any. The social workers never came looking for me. I slept outside the first few days, and I was lucky it was summer. Eventually, I met Sarah. She hung around the streets, but not as a hooker or anything like that, but to give people sandwiches and stuff. She knew I was new to the streets and was young. I told her my story.

She felt bad that life didn't even give me a chance, so she told me I can live with her but had to work at her store. Sarah seemed like someone I could trust and so I followed her home that day like a damn stray dog looking for something to eat and a place to sleep.

Sarah owned a used clothing store in the downtown area of Regina. She told me about it as we drove home to her house. She lived in the downtown area in a small house that was not fancy or anything, but I wasn't going to complain. I found the deal a hell of a lot better than huddling behind a garbage bin to try to sleep. It was better than hanging around behind the Chinese restaurant alleyway waiting for leftovers to be chucked out so I could eat. I moved in with Sarah and stayed with her for two years. Sarah was good to me. She once lived on the streets after her husband kicked her out. She had no money and no real education. She shared her story of being a drunk on the streets of Regina. She said her whole life was about drinking and living just to drink. She said this one time, she ended up in the hospital after she almost drank herself to death. She sobered up and went back to Thunder Bay, Ontario to live with her elderly father. She said her dad died a few years later and left her with a few dollars. Anyways, Sarah had enough to come back and open her little clothing shop. She vowed to try to help others out. She knew their struggles. Sarah had a good heart. Sarah was a mixed blood woman. She said her dad was white and her mom was a beautiful Mohawk woman. Sarah looked like she was beautiful too at one time, but the booze stole the physical beauty and left her with some drunk scars on her face. Her heart was pure gold and more beautiful than anything. She was a strong woman too. Sarah taught me that I could make it on my own. Sarah was the peace I really needed in my life and for a while I actually started to believe that maybe a God did exist and sent me to Sarah. That two years of peace, thinking, and planning was good for me and soon I was feeling strong enough to leave and try life out on my own. I decided I would leave that summer after I turned seventeen. I loved living with Sarah, but I really didn't want her to think I was using her for her house and job. I was like that. I never really wanted to go through life owning anybody anything. I guess owing meant I would have to pay back, and paying back kinda meant that someone else owned a part of me. I didn't want that. The day I left Sarah was a sad day, but it was a day I knew was coming. I decided to take the first bus that was scheduled out of Regina, and this was how I ended up in Edmonton,

So, there you have it, the early years of Stella.

I read my first chapter to Mr. Evans today. I was once told that even when people were dying, the last thing to go was their hearing. I want to believe that and so I made a promise to myself that I would read to Mr. Evans each time I write. Not that he is dying or anything, but in a sense, being in a coma is like living without really living. At least that is how I see it. Anyways, I decided I will read to him 'cause just maybe he can hear my stories. Maybe he can't, but just in case he can, I want to share them with him. I guess it also gives me practice on reading and checking my own writing. For me, I just want to write like I am right there talking to people who are reading, so I figure if I hear my own voice, I will know for sure how the story is going. I want my writing to feel like I am telling a story. Just like when I sit and have tea with Mrs. Evans, I just talk and tell her stories. I think practicing my reading and writing on Mr. Evans is real good too 'cause he can't tell me if it is bad or good. He is just a good listener, and this is all I want for now. This one time, though, when I was reading that part about my mom and dad dying, I am sure I seen a tear roll down Mr. Evans's eye. I sometimes just sit and stare at him, thinking that at any moment, he will wake up. I'm not trying to be creepy like that, but I think just maybe my stories will wake him up. Once I told myself that Mr. Evans really can hear me, I decided that I would not focus too much on the bad stuff and maybe write about the crazy stuff I done. Maybe if I make him laugh, he will want to wake up. His wife misses him so much. Heck, even I miss him.

CRAZY DAYS OF SUMMER

Summer seemed to be the time of many crazy memories. Maybe it was the hot weather that had people do crazy things. After I left Regina, I made my way to Edmonton. I was seventeen years old. I had never been to Edmonton before but had heard people talk about it. I am not sure if it was chance that had me on that bus, or why things turned out the way they did, but I believe it was my good rule that helped me along the way. That rule was that when I walked into the bus station, I would hop the next scheduled bus out of Regina. It worked out that it would be the bus to Edmonton. I had heard many stories about this big-ass-crazy-ass mall that was in Edmonton. It was supposed to be the biggest mall in the world. Imagine that. In the whole wide world, it was the biggest one and I just happened to get on the bus that was headed that way. I had made it my goal to go and see it since I was headed there anyways. I left Sarah's house with a couple thousand dollars I had managed to save. Well, truth be said, she managed to save it for me, so I wasn't too worried about money just yet. And I think in the back of my mind, I knew I could always head back to Sarah's place in Regina if this being-on-my-own thing didn't work out.

I spent my first night in a motel on the outskirts of Edmonton. Luckily for me, the bus ended up having a flat tire and had to pull over. A small motel sat where we stopped, and I figured it was a good stop for me, seeing as I was only seventeen and so it wasn't going to be easy to get a room. This place looked empty, and I knew empty meant they would take anyone that just walked in. There was a coffee shop where most of us went and sat while the bus was getting fixed, and it was there I made the decision to maybe spend the night. It was my first night away as a grown up, and as much thinking I did about living life out on my own, I didn't really think about the reality of it all. I guess in my mind, I pretended it was as easy as just walking into the great big world, getting a job, making money, my own place, some new friends, and boom, things would just work out. Yes, it certainly sounded real easy in my mind, but the truth was, without anyone really to help me along, I knew it was going to be harder than what I thought. Up until then, I had help along the way. Some help I didn't want, could do without, but it was still a somebody guiding me. I guess in a way, I was lucky in having others kind of tell me what to do, but now, reality had slapped my fat ass. I had to come up with a real plan before moving on. The hotel wasn't a bad place—not really clean—but nice enough. By the end of the night, I learned it was a common stop for many travelers, and it was the place I met my first real friend in the big real world. I met Donna that night. She was stopping in for the night too before heading to her Reserve nearby. I knew of Indian Reserves, but 'cause my foster situations were never on the Reserves, I didn't know a whole bunch. I had just learned in school about the Treaties and how Indian people were put on the Reserves. I didn't really learn about the truth about land being stolen from us Indians but knew that many of us were put on Reserves as a way to control us. I also knew I was from one but never really thought about going back there. I think I made myself believe that Birch Creek didn't exist anymore—that it died the day we got taken away. I guess if it was gone in my mind, I wouldn't think to go back. Not going back was my way of sparing myself the heartache.

Donna was like me, brown skin and all. I always felt pretty good when I met brown skins like me. Somehow, there was a connection that I can't really describe. They were like home without really going to a home. I don't know, it's hard to describe. Anyways, she tells me she's going home after being away for ten years. Her mom passed away, and she was headed home to say her goodbyes. She said her mom had a house on the Reserve and that maybe she would stay awhile to clean it, and maybe live there just until she figured stuff out.

That night, Donna and I share a six-pack of beer, and after two, I am feeling giggly and full of stories. Donna too shares her story with me. She had moved to Vancouver many years ago with her boyfriend. They had a fairy-tale love. She met him at a rodeo in Calgary and fell instantly in love with him. She said she loved that cowboy look, that cowboy smell. I wasn't really sure what that cowboy smell was, but in time, I too did get a whiff. Anyways, Donna goes on to tell me that she ended up marrying her cowboy but now lived alone 'cause her husband had passed away a few years back. She said he was a semitruck driver and was found in a hotel in the United States somewhere. They figure he had a heart attack. Donna said she liked Vancouver and decided to stay and live there 'cause there was nothing at the Rez (that's what she called it) for her to go home to besides her brothers and her mom. But now that her mom was gone, she felt bad she didn't go home sooner.

Donna was a good storyteller too, so her and I stay up real late sharing stories. She had driven from Vancouver and had decided to spend the night at the motel we met at. I am glad she stopped 'cause I felt I had made myself a real friend. By the end of the night, she gives me a few phone numbers I can call if I want to reach her. I share my story with her too and explain that I was on my way to Edmonton to visit the West Edmonton Mall. Donna tells me she can drop me off at the West Edmonton Mall in the morning on her way out of town. This was a good friend indeed, and my first night living on my own as an adult wasn't looking too bad.

The next morning, Donna and I head to the world's biggest mall. I was so excited to see it. As we drive closer, I can see a tall, tall building. There is parking all over, and thousands and thousands of vehicles. She drops me off with my backpack of possessions at one of entranceways and tells me to stay in touch. She tells me she is only three hours away, so if I wanted to catch up with her later, to either bus it or hitch to Chief Meetos Reserve. I stood there watching her drive away, wondering if she and I would ever meet again. Little did I know that Donna would be a part of my life for many years to come.

I sit and read about Donna to Mr. Evans. I really wanted him to know what a good friend she had been to me. Again, like the last time, it appeared that there was some sort of eye movement as I read to him. Excited, I tell the nurse about it, and she explains that the nerves have a way of making things move in our bodies, making it seem like something is happening. She tells me not to read too much into it. She tells me to prepare myself for the fact that Mr. Evans may never wake up again. Of course, I had my own ideas about that, and her having the nursing papers didn't really change my mind where Mr. Evans was concerned. I believe that he could hear me, and I promised to keep reading to him for as long as I was writing.

When Mrs. Evans came in later that day, I told her that Mr. Evans seemed to have extra eye movement each time I read to him. Like the nurse, she didn't seem to think anything of it either. I think deep down inside she wanted to believe what I believed, but she was saving her hopes from getting shattered. She went with what the nurse was telling us, and I found it sad not to share in the hope. I think at that point, I really felt sorry for Mrs. Evans. I know in her heart she wanted so badly to have him back but was scared to hang on to that hope 'cause it might just break her heart more in the end. I could see her point in more ways than I thought. I guess that was why I didn't look behind each time I left a place. Maybe I needed to understand why I never looked back too; behind me was another story that I just wasn't willing to face quite yet either. I decided that this reading thing would be just between me and Mr. Evans. It was only fair I didn't get Judy's hope up in case he never did wake up. Plus, I really liked reading to him, it made him seem, well, less dead, I guess.

ANYWAYS, BACK TO THE WEST EDMONTON MALL...

The mall—it was everything I heard it was. It was big, big, big. There were stores and people, and more stores, and more people. There was even a fair in that mall with a big roller coaster. It even had a great big swimming pool that looked like a beach. It was crazy, crazy, crazy. I just couldn't believe I was in the mall. It was so big. I walked for what seemed like hours, trying to see everything. The mall was a fascinating place and I thought I could live there forever. I knew, of course, that was not possible, so I thought of the next best thing, and that would try find work there. I spent the day walking from store to store asking for a job. Again, people showed me just how rude they could be. Most of them just shooed me away like I was a bum off the street. And

I guess in a sense they were right. **But really!** They can be nicer about it. I think I tried almost every store I thought I would have a chance at and even tried them fancy restaurants and fast-food joints. Still no luck with a job. I decide to leave the mall later that evening, hoping to find a place to crash. I decide to jump in a taxi and tell the driver to drive me to a cheap motel. He drives me back to the one I stayed at the night before. I decide I really have to think of a real plan 'cause I knew my money wasn't going to last me forever. As it was, I was being real cheap just to make it last longer, but staying in a motel was costing me.

I get back to the motel and go to the front desk. I explain to the lady my situation. She gives me a room key but tells me that maybe Edmonton was not a good place for me to be. Said I was too young to be out on my own. I tell her my story, and she says she is sorry. She tells me again that Edmonton would not be a good fit for me. I decide I would hitchhike to Chief Meetos Reserve the next morning to find Donna.

I remember waking up early, butterflies in my gut. It was scary to be hitchhiking to places I had never been. I remember heading out to the road early that morning after asking the front desk guy the directions to the Chief Meetos Reserve. I stood out there for six hours before this guy stops and asks me where I am headed. I tell him I am trying to go home to see my family, that there'd been a death, and I needed to get home. I don't know why I lied to him, but I guess I figured if I tell him that, he would feel sorry for me and give me a ride. Besides, it was only half a lie since there really was a death of a family member—just not mine. My natural instinct to survive was kicking in, and I soon realized that this was going to be the way to survive. The guy gives me a ride and asks me a bunch of questions about my life. I didn't want to get caught in my lying, so I just tell him that I couldn't talk right now, as every time I think about home, I want to cry. He stays quiet the rest of the way and cranks the tunes on his stereo. The ride was nice. The tunes were pretty good too. He drops me off at the turn and tells me it's a few kilometers walk in.

I look at him and say, "I know, I'm from here, remember?"

As he pulled out to leave, he waves at me and says, "See you around, Rachel."

Not really sure where I had gotten the name from, but as my lies to survive went on, Rachel was a name I do remember using frequently. Plus, I figured I better stick with one fake name 'cause I sure didn't want to get caught in my own bullshitting. I wave at him and look down the road to my next adventure.

I remember walking the few kilometers in to the "Rez," as Donna would call it, and coming upon a small building which looked more like a house than anything. The first thing I noticed about the house was there was a gas pump outside along with a pay phone booth. I figured I had better call one of the numbers Donna had given me to tell her that I had taken her up on her offer to come out here. I wasn't sure about the choice I had made at the time but was sure glad I had met her and had someone to turn to when I needed. It was nice to meet people like that. I found her at the first number I called, and she instructed me to stay at the store and said she would send her cousin Carrot to come pick me up. Yeah, I know, Carrot. I giggled too when he introduced himself. A few weeks into meeting him, I learned why they called him that. Anyways, Carrot and I drove to where Donna was staying. She was at her late mother's house. I felt bad for showing up during this time of someone dying. Carrot walked in with me, and I was glad he did. There were a lot of people at the house, and I sure felt out of place and actually kind of stupid for showing up at such a bad time. But somehow, everyone there made me feel welcome. I had never been to a place that had only brown skins, and I will admit, it felt real good. It felt like I was home but within myself. I helped Donna out those few days with cooking and cleaning. I had never been to a funeral before, and sadly, I did not even get to attend the funerals of my mom and dad. Donna's mother was named Marie, like my late mother, and so I took this as a sign that somehow Donna and I were supposed to meet.

I ended up staying at Chief Meetos Reserve that summer. It was my first summer on my own and the summer for many firsts. Donna left for Vancouver shortly after her mother's funeral but returned to the Rez later that summer. She asked me to house sit while she tried to figure out what to do with her mother's house.

Some of my most memorable moments happened that summer at Chief Meetos, and one night in particular included losing my virginity to Carrot. By this time, I had become used to drinking beer, and really, that was all I stuck with until I moved to the larger cities. Anyways, this one night, shortly after Donna left, a bunch of us had gotten together to celebrate someone's birthday. We made a big campfire outside someone's house. I honestly do not remember who it was. It was so long ago. Anyways, I remember a bunch of us sitting around the fire drinking and singing. One guy had a guitar and thought he was the Conway Twitty of the bunch. It had started to rain, so the party was coming to a close, and it was already morning. I recall Carrot asking me if I needed someone to walk me home, and I said that it would be nice. The houses were spread apart, not lined up like them city houses, and so going from one house to the next was not a hop, skip, and a jump. Except in my case, this time it was a hop, a step back, and a hump. I was drunk.

We got into the house and Carrot asked if he could just crash there. And boom, just like that, I grabbed him and started to kiss him. I had kissed before but had never done the deed. I don't know if I was desperate to know what it felt like, or if it was the booze doing its work, but I grabbed him and told him to come sleep with me. He didn't say no. Once in bed, I told him that I had never done sex in my life, and he said he'd be gentle with me. What happened next, I will never forget. Anyways, Carrot gets on top, very gently slides his thingy into me, and starts his humping motion. The first few seconds kind of hurt, then it stopped. After he was done, he falls over, thingy hanging out and asks how it was. I tell him that I had expected it to hurt more, 'cause I had learned in Sex Ed class that the first time was to hurt real bad. By this time, it was daylight, and I was able to see everything. I turned to him and looked between his legs. And there it was. A carrot shaped thingy. Wiener. Now, I know I was no expert at looking at ding dongs, but I was pretty sure they normally didn't look like that. I learned that night why they called him Carrot. We both fell asleep, and the next morning, I told Carrot that I'm sorry for bringing him to my bed. He tells me that he likes me and wants to be my boyfriend, but all I could think of was his carrot. I don't know, I think I was mean, but I just couldn't date a guy with a carrot wiener. It was not like the guys were lining up, but still.

When Donna returned later that summer, things got pretty heated. Donna could party, fight, and drink. I was her sidekick. Anyways, this one night, we hitchhike to the local farm town, 'cause Donna didn't want to drive knowing we were going to drink. She takes me to this bar for us to go sit and enjoy a night out. Everything was going real good. We met up with a couple others from the Rez, and we sit down with them to have a few drinks. After the first two, I need to piss, so I get up and walk toward the bathroom. As I walk past the bar, this one white is sitting there on one of them bar stools. I walk by and just as I breeze past him, he yells, "Hey, who let the squaw in?"

Well, shit, I don't know what the hell came over me. I turn around and punch that fucker right in the mouth, knocking him off his bar stool. The little shit must have weighted a hundred pounds, and I sure wasn't scared of him. Anyway, Donna sees what's happening, jumps up, and comes running over. The guy is on the floor, but this don't stop Donna from kneeling down and punching him in the face. Two minutes later, Donna and I are being hauled out by a few of the guys that work there. I had forgotten I needed to pee, but once the commotion stopped and we were outside, my bladder reminded me that it needed to be emptied. I tell Donna I need to pee real bad, so she tells me to go behind the bar. I walk behind and squat, not paying attention to who was around. I get up and half stagger to the front. Just as I was halfway around the bar, I am stopped by a police officer. He tells me I am under arrest for peeing in a public place. He grabs me and cuffs me. I am screaming for Donna, who at this point I lose sight of and is nowhere to be seen. I kind of panic now 'cause I had never been to jail before and we are in a town that is not very friendly to brown skins. Anyways, the cop throws me in the back of his car, where low and behold, I find Donna already sitting there. I figured that if I was going down, at least someone was coming with me. I ask Donna what the hell is going on, and she tells me they nabbed her while I was out taking a piss. Anyways, Donna tells me not to talk to no one. She tells me the cops don't like us Indians, and are always looking for a reason to arrest us. We get driven about thirty minutes out to the nearest drunk tank. Donna and I spent the night together in a cell. The next morning, an officer comes and tells us that we will both be charged for assault. I get an extra charge for peeing in a public place. I try explaining my story to the cop, but he tells me to save it for the judge. We get released later that morning and are given a court date. Since our court is scheduled for fall, Donna tells me she's not going to worry bout it 'cause by fall she would be halfway to Vancouver. She tells me to maybe come up with an exit plan too.

I learned the ways of the crazy world that summer with Donna. This one night, she throws a big party at her house. Anyways, there is little man called Skunk. Seemed everyone on the Rez has nicknames, which I thought was pretty cool. Thing was, the nickname tells something about a person's character. Skunk, well, he got his name when he was little. Guess the poor little guy would get lice all the time 'cause he had real thick black hair. His mom would pour peroxide down the middle to kill the bugs. This would 'cause the middle to go blonde and so the other kids just called him Skunk. Anyway, we were partying, and Skunk passes out real fast. I learned so much about Donna that summer, and one thing I learned was she was not just a fighter, but a joker too. Well, Skunk, he's out cold, and Donna says we are going to have some fun with him. She gets him up off the couch he's sleeping on and drags him to the kitchen. Skunk—he sleeps through the whole thing. She continues to drag him under the table and gets some rope and ties each limb to the table. So, poor Skunk, he's now tied up, spread eagle under the table. Donna proceeds to pull his socks off, but not completely off, just enough so that they're hanging off his feet. Donna picks up a lighter and lights his sock on fire. Well Skunk musta felt the heat 'cause he tries to move, and realizes he's tied up. Now the whole damn table is shaking real good, and everyone is killing themselves laughing at Skunk. One guy, he laughs so hard, he shits himself. So now we have smelly burnt socks and shit in the house. Skunk don't talk to us for a while on a count of what Donna did to him.

There was a lot these kinds of pranks done to people who couldn't hold their booze. Another time, this lady—I'll call her Maggie, 'cause I honestly forgot her real name. But anyways, Maggie comes over to Donna's house. By the time she showed up, she'd been drinking pretty hard, so it don't take long for her to pass out. It had been a hot day, so everyone had been sitting outside. It was early in the day—midafternoon—and me and Donna had spent the morning doing some yard cleaning and was planning a cookout. Anyways, Maggie, she shows up with a case of beer and says she wants to drink with us. We stop cleaning for a bit and decide to sit and have one with her. Well, she doesn't even finish her beer and she's sleeping, passed out cold. I tell Donna that Maggie looks hot wearing them pants and thick sweater, so Donna tells me to go inside to grab scissors. I bring her back the scissors, hand them to her, and she says, "Well you know what to do with them"

Fact was, I really didn't know what to do, so I take it upon myself to guess at what Donna was thinking I should do. Meanwhile, as Donna was just getting ready to go into the shed, she hands me some string. I was still confused, but kind of had an idea on what she was expecting, so I took the scissors and cut Maggie's pant legs off, making her a pair of short shorts. I had just finished cutting her sweater into a short shirt when Donna came running back holding a tarp yelling, "Stella, what the hell are you doing?"

"I thought you wanted me to air condition her by cutting her shorts and shirt," I reply, still holding the string in my hand. Well Donna, she falls over laughing, holding the tarp, hardly able to talk. In between her laughing fit she finally tells me that she was trying to make shade for Maggie and thought I knew to cut the rope into pieces so we can tie the tarp over. Holy shit, I couldn't fricking believe what I did that to that poor lady.

The summer at Chief Meetos seemed to go by so fast. Mostly Donna and I got along, but this one incident almost cost us our friendship. I was making so many friends on the Rez, it felt good to have people in my life, and I think I almost forgot how I got there in the first place and, it was on the count of Donna. I almost blew it too. I really messed up on this one thing, and I almost lose everything. This is how it happened. Anyways, we went back to that little farm town with the bar, except this time Donna brings backup. She tells her three cousins that we had a bit of trouble the last time we went, and now we even have court dates 'cause of it. So, she asks George to be our driver and tells her other cousins to come along too. Just in case, you know? We get to the bar, and everything goes good at the first like the last time. We sit and have our drinks. We don't bother no one. After a few, me and Donna get up to dance. While we are dancing, that little shit disturber I almost knocked out the last time come up to us and now starts calling me and Donna "lezzies." I didn't care what he called me, but the fact that he was in my face every time—I tell him to get lost, and he gets worse. Anyways, the dam dummy keeps calling us "lezzies" to the point that he goes and just pisses Donna right off too. Donna don't like being called any names by anyone. I could tell she is trying to keep her cool 'cause she just wants to have a good time and dance. Anyways, she gets fed up with that sawed-off-little-half-twit and clocks the fucker right then and there on the dance floor. Little shit hits the floor real hard, face first, and now there is blood everywhere. The guy's on the floor crying and rolling around, holding his nose. We try to head out the door real fast as to not cause any more trouble but, them fucking pig cops are already at the door waiting for us. They grab Donna and cuff her, leaving the rest of us behind. The one cop looks at us and tells us to best leave the place before any more trouble start. And that's how it was! Blame the Indians when shit went down! But now we got ourselves a situation and were stuck wondering what the hell to do, so George says we best go to the station to see what they are going to do with Donna. He says maybe they'll hand her to him since he was sober and all.

We get to the station and George tells us to stay and wait in the vehicle—that he'll go in alone. We wait for about ten minutes, and George comes out and tells us that Donna can be released on a five hundred dollar bail. He says Donna has the money covered, but we'd have to drive back to the Rez and get it. Well, we are just about to leave when Jolene, Donna's cousin, decides we should pick up a case of beer for the drive home. It's not that late, so we figure, why not? We go to drive home, but now George starts to drink too, so by the time we get back to the Rez, he's half cut and feeling no pain. We head straight to Donna's house to go get the cash. George goes in the house to find the money that Donna stashed, and he brings it out with him. George gets back in the car, and we head back to pick up Donna. Halfway there, George says how that beer tasted real good on our way back to the Rez, and how he wished he had some more. He says he has cash of his own and wants to make a quick stop at the bar to have a quick drink before we pick up Donna. We tell him that we aren't going in with him, and he's on his own, so he tells us he will have just one and come right back out. Like a bunch of idiots, we believe him and hang back at the car and have a smoke while we wait. Anyways, we wait for George in the car for about twenty minutes or so, but he's taking too dam long. I tell the ladies that I will go in and check on him only to find him with an old ex of his, trying to smooth things over with her. He was just sitting there sipping on a beer like he had no one waiting on him. I tell him to hurry 'cause we got to go get Donna out. He tells me to sit and have a beer with them and I figure that maybe if I did, he would leave soon. I tell him, "Just one, George, then we are leaving!"

Well, as the story goes, that first one led to another, then another. And then of course, another. Next thing I know, the ladies come from the car and join the party and we drink up the bail money. Donna, well, she was pissed! She spent three days in that cell cause of the previous charges, plus the assault that was pending from the half-twit. Poor Donna ends up hitchhiking home when she gets out, comes straight home, and kicks me out of her place.

I walked to Carrot's house that day, not really knowing what to do. Fortunately, Carrot still lived with his mother, so he really couldn't try to play me. His mother was the Jesus-loving kind, so shacking up would have been a no-no, which worked for me

’cause I wasn’t interested in Carrot that way. Carrot’s mom—she let me stay there, but she also tells me that it can’t be long term. I lay low for a couple days, then go back to Donna’s to beg for forgiveness. **She tells me that the only thing we could all do was to pay her back the $500 we drank up that night, plus interest.** I tell her I would come up with a plan.

QUICK CASH JOBS AND OTHER SCAMS

As I read to Mr. Evans, I was reminded about how I felt that day Donna kicked me out. It scared me something bad, and I think it was when I finally figured out that I really had to learn to look after myself better. That maybe depending on people to look out for me was not such a good idea. I really had no schooling too, so I had to use my street skills to think of ways to look after myself. I felt safe right now, and looking down at the sleeping Mr. Evans, I felt proud that I made it this far in looking after myself. I have my own little place, and I feed myself. I don't ever have to worry about anyone kicking me out again. I mean, yeah, I deserved it when Donna kicked me out cause what we did was wrong, but still, I think it was a good lesson for me to learn. Maybe somehow it was all part of the "plan." I didn't get too attached to places and people after that summer with Donna. I had friends, but if they left, or I had to leave, there was no strings attached.

I guess getting kicked out by someone I really cared for set me straight on stuff like that. Had the idea that no one was going to ever kick me out again and made damn sure I left town before anyone could try. Anyway, I was young when I first met Donna, and I relied too much on people to look out for me. I grew up and got better at looking after myself, but I never had a good break like the one I had here with the Evans. I look down at sleeping Mr. Evans, and I thank him and his wife for giving me a chance here. This was one job I wanted to hang on to for as long as I could. Life was getting better. **The "plan" was getting better.**

Anyways, back to my story about me and George. Me and George, well, we both didn't work, and we knew that Donna meant her word when she said, "five hundred bucks plus interest, assholes. That's what you owe me for my troubles. So, get that dam money to me soon."

I got scared of her when she said that 'cause I can see the madness in her eyes too. George and I sit down and have a meeting later that afternoon about how we going to come up with the five hundred we owe Donna. George says that there are lots of farms close to the Rez, and maybe we could act like them Udderites and steal chickens, then come sell them on the Rez. He tells me he done it before and made some serious fast cash. Man, I didn't know what to think of his plan, but I didn't like it. He tells me that I can be the lookout and stay in the vehicle. Only problem was, George and I have no vehicle either. But good ol' George had a plan for that too. He tells me that getting a vehicle was the easy part, and he would look after that. Apparently, the Rez had a van they used for emergencies, so he tells me he would have the van by the next day. Well, George made good on the van, and I don't even bother to ask what kind of emergency he lied about to get the van. I figured the less I knew about his lies, the better off for me. Next thing I know, George and I are parked on a back road to a farm and waiting for it to get dark. As soon as it gets a little dark, George tells me that "operation chicken steal" is on. He tells me the chickens are close to the yard, so he says we are going to fake a break down. He tells me it's too risky to just go into the yard unnoticed. He tells me to go in and ask for help but to speak an Indian language 'cause if they don't understand me, it will be easier to fool them. I tell George I had no idea what my language was and what it even sounded like, but I'd try to fake one anyway. He tells me that he'll loosens the battery cable and make sure the van is dead in case someone comes out to help me. I do as I am told, but as I leave, I find an old scarf in the van and wrap my head to try to make myself look older. I go knock on the door. A man answers it, and I start talking, "Chimmy ona kayak."

While I'm talking, I use my hands and pretend I am driving a vehicle and start point to the road. The man tells me politely he can't understand me, so I try real hard to bring tears to my eyes and act like I am stressed. This time, while waving my hands like a mad woman, I say, "Kippa shena daya moon chi. Kimpa ola mega chinsa." (Well, I don't actually remember what I really said, but trust me, it sounded real good at the time.)

Again, the man said he could not understand me, so I start to cry. I figured crying would buy me some time, and quite honestly, I am not sure where the damn tears come from, but they come anyway. I finish crying, and I point to the man's jacket and boots and motion him to come outside with me. I am not sure what George is doing, but I was praying he don't get caught. Anyway, the guy must figure I am harmless, puts on his boots and jacket, and follows me out. I walk him to the road and point at the van. As we are walking, I look around for George 'cause I don't want him getting caught, but I don't see him anywhere. The man gets into the van and tries to start it. Of course, the van is dead, so he gets out and pops the hood to look under. He has his flashlight with him, so he starts shining it all over the motor until he comes to the battery. He starts fidgeting with the battery and tries his best to tighten the cable. Now, I am sitting in the driver seat acting like I drove the dam thing, and he motions me to turn the key. I turn it, and the damn thing starts. I jump out of the vehicle and go hug him while ranting, "Joma home oka cheese," or something like that. I make like he's a hero and that he just saved my life. The man closes the hood and I bow to him in thanks. He doesn't talk to me but walks away while I crawl back into the driver's seat pretending that I am ready to drive away.

While I am sitting there, George comes running out of the bush with a bunch of dead chickens in his arms. He throws them in the back of the van, and we take off. He tells me we need to hit a few more farms, but I tell him I am not liking his idea and that it would take too long to come up with the money. I tell him I got an idea too, but we would need the van for a few days, and we needed to get to a bigger city where no one would know us. He tells me we have enough gas to get to Edmonton, which was three hours away. Anyway, we drive into the night, and just outside of Edmonton, we sleep in a van full of dead chickens. For my plan, I tell George we will need a gas can. We stop at a gas station with a garage and George sees a gas can inside. He tells me to keep the guy busy so he can steal it for us. I go in and act like I'm in great pain, holding my stomach. The guy asks me if I am okay, and I tell him I need a bathroom real bad. I tell him I think I ate something bad and was ready to be sick. (And you gotta remember I was young, and I was a pretty good-looking brown skin. The guy looked like he a pervert, so he be as helpful as possible). Anyways, I go to the bathroom and make a bunch of puking noises so the guy hears me. He stays standing on the other side of the door, asking now and then if I amokay. I wash my face and come out, trying to look like I just had a real good puke. I tell him I feel better and thank him. I jump back into the van where George is waiting with the gas can, and we take off.

I tell him to drive to the West Edmonton Mall parking lot. We park the van, and I go to the other side of the parking lot while holding the gas can. I walk around, looking for people who look like they are not so cheap, and tell them that I have run out of gas and that I need money to fill my gas can to get home. It takes me four hours to come up with three hundred bucks. Easy money. I go back to the van where George is waiting, and we decide to head back to the Rez. Of course, we use some of the money to buy gas for the van, but at least we got a down payment for Donna, two hundred and forty bucks to be exact. Donna, well, she takes the money and tells us we still owe her. Anyway, the funny part of this story is, we get back to the Rez, and we forget we have a van full of dead chickens. George, he goes and gives the van back, and he doesn't take out the chickens. A few days later, George gets a call from some lady who tells him that he can never borrow the van again.

George and me—well, now we are still short about three hundred dollars 'cause of Donna wanting interest and all, so we try to think of other ways to come up with the money. George tells me that he knows who the bootlegger is and says that fastest way to make money is to sell booze. He says that if we steal the guy's stash, he can't call the cops 'cause what he's doing is not legal anyways. Except this job would be a lot harder than the last two. I go along with him and ask what I can do. George smiles at me real sneaky, and I think that I am not going to like his plan.

He tells me, "Okay Stella, you gotta act like you're lost and go ask Ol' Kenny for directions. Ol' Kenny there, well he like his girls young, so you go knocking on his door, act real cute, and show him some tits. Got that?"

Well, I don't like that plan one bit, and I tell George I ain't taking my pants off for some old man but tell him I will go along with it anyways for Donna. George tells me not to worry 'cause it won't get that far and says he will come in after he steals the booze, and all I have to do is get Ol' Kenny to the bedroom. He says that once Ol' Kenny is in the bedroom, he will sneak in and go steal the booze. Then, he would come back and rescue me. Well, the plan sounds pretty good, so I go along with it but dreaded my role in the whole thing.

I go knocking on Ol' Kenny's door, and when he yells for me to come in, I walk in and act like I'm lost. He sees me standing by the door and quickly gets up off his couch to come talk to me. I quickly unbutton the top buttons on my shirt to give the old guy a bit of a show. When he comes close, I ask him if he knew where Donna lives, and he says Donna is down the road. I tell him I am thirsty and ask him for a drink of water. While I am drinking, I spill water on myself and tell Kenny that my shirt is all wet and ask to borrow one of his. I take my shirt off right then and there, and smile at him. I get real close to him now and ask him again if he got a shirt in his bedroom I can use. He tells me he does, and as he's walking away from me, I take my cup of water and throw at his pants. I giggle and tell him he better take his pant off. Ol' Kenny, well, he's beside himself now thinking he's got this in the bag and rips his pant off right then and there. I walk up to him and put my hand on his thigh and stoke it. Now Ol' Kenny touches my hair, and I just want to puke, but I keep playing 'cause I know I am doing this for Donna. I tell him to go lay on the bed and that I would take good care of him. He walks to his bed and as he's going, he takes off his gitch and exposes his saggingold ass. He turns around to look at me, and if ever I had to keep a poker face, it was now. Man, I just wanted to throw up right then and there looking at them old prune balls, just hanging. But I keep my cool and take my eyes off his wrinkled old body and look for a distraction. I see a radio sitting on his shelf, so I motion myself towards it, and turn it on. There was no way I was going to crawl into his bed, so I play him for as long as I can, hoping that George is now in the house stealing the booze. I start singing to a song that is playing on the radio and act like I am going to give it to him real good. Ol' Kenny, well, he starts rubbing the bed and tells me to join him. By this time, I am sick to my stomach, and I tell him that I need to pee. I leave him in the bedroom, and as I am walking to the bathroom, I spot George sneaking out the door with a case of whiskey in his arms. I knew that I was in the clear, so I run after him. And Ol' Kenny, well, **I leave him half naked in his bedroom with them dirty ol' balls waiting for action they never going to get.**

It didn't take long for Ol' Kenny to come knocking on Donna's door saying I stole his stash. George just happened to be sitting at the table when Ol' Kenny come by, and tells him to call the cops, then laughs. Ol' Kenny tells George that he will shoot him if he ever came into his yard again. George, of course, just laugh at him and says that maybe someone is trying to clean up the bootlegging on the Rez. He smiles at me, and I say nothing. By the end of the week, George sells the booze and gets the rest of our money to pay back Donna. **Our debt was paid in full!** I truly believe that George was my master trainer in the art of scams, 'cause I became pretty good at them for years to come.

I look down at Mr. Evans as I am reading this part of my book and tell him not to worry 'cause them days are gone now that I have a job and everything's going good. I tell him that he and his wife been too good to me for me to do anything like that. In case he was hearing all my stories, I didn't want him to get stressed or anything. Mr. Evans just lay there looking at peace, like he's trusting in me. And he should, 'cause that was the old Stella, and that Stella was on pause for now. I tell Mr. Evans several times that I am a better person now 'cause of him and Judy. I wanted him to believe me, but even more, I wanted to believe me.

Anyways, for years, I had to rely on scamming to get by, to eat. This one time, I had already settled in Vancouver, and my buddies and I had been on a four-day binge. Anyways, there was some kind of music festival happening. We lived close to the area and had woken up pretty hung over. Well, my buddy Daniel, he was working for some construction company at the time, and he had just gotten fired. Anyways, Daniel kept them orange little working vests with him and tells me he still has three at his place. He says that we should go down to the festival 'cause he has an idea. So, we clean ourselves up—Daniel, Jimmy Nine-Toes, and me. We wash up so we don't look hung over, and we head to Daniel's place to grab the vests.

Daniel's an artist too, and has all kinds of paper and stuff, so he quickly makes a big sign that says, "Parking $5 all day."

We get down to the festival before too many people arrive, and Jimmy Nine-Toes knocks over the free parking sign and hides it. They tell me to go and direct the cars to where they are to park, and they would stand at the entrance and collect fees. They send the first six cars to me without trouble, and the next car asks why there was free parking the day before. Jimmy, well, he gets a little bit hotheaded and starts to swear at the guy, and so Daniel waves me over to get out. We run, leaving Jimmy 'cause we know pretty damn soon the cops are going to show up. Anyways, we get around the block, and Daniel is laughing that he made thirty bucks in ten minutes. Had it not been for Jimmy, we could have had more money. Anyways, we became pretty good at the parking scam, and did a few more after that.

The early '80s was prime time for cheque scams. This one time, I had gotten really sick and had to go to the walk-in emergency room. Anyways, while I am waiting in the lobby, I wanted to puke real bad. I mean, I am sick. Real sick. So anyway, I run to the bathroom, and I'm pounding on the door, trying to get in real fast, yelling I am about to puke. This lady comes scrambling out real fast, forgetting her purse in the bathroom. At first, I don't notice, but when I was done and getting ready to clean myself, I notice the purse sitting on the floor. I decide to keep up the puking noise and dig to see what she have. I find a chequebook, so I take the last five cheques in the back. I figure she won't notice them gone. I stuff the cheques in my pocket and go hand the lady back her purse. Of course, the old bag starts rifling through her stuff checking to see if I stole from her. She finds all her money still there and don't even bother to check her chequebook. When I get home later that day, I try to figure out how I am going to use the cheques. A few days later, I go into the Army and Navy store and buy a bunch of clothes. I use a cheque to pay and sign my name, Harriet Francis. The cashier, she don't even question me. I take the stuff home. A few days later, I go back to the Army and Navy store and tell them I don't want the clothes and ask for my money back. They pay me back in cash.

Long time ago, they never had no cameras or anything, so sometimes, I would go into the Army and Navy store and "try on" shirts. Anyways, I would tell the dressing room lady I have four shirts but really, I have two others hidden in them. I put two on under my shirt and go back and hand her the four I told her I had, then tell her they don't fit. I would sell the shirts for a reduced price later. Another real good Army and Navy scam I had was the receipt game. This scam required a "helper" as I would call them 'cause in the end, they really were helping me survive. I would stand outside the Army and Navy store waiting for someone that looked scam-able. I would then approach them and tell them that I worked for an organization that helped kids. I would explain that if they gave me their receipt, the store would match their purchase and would send a donation for that amount to the kids in need. I know, I know, not cool, but I figured them commercials on TV were scamming too, so if they could, why couldn't I? And it only really worked a few times. But what I would do then is use one of my old Army and Navy bags and go and fill the bag with whatever was on the receipts. I would then go to the return desk and tell some crazy story about how my money was stolen by my brother, and that he come into the store to buy crap, and now I was just looking to get my money back. Again, like I said before, I only done this a couple of times. And surprisingly, it worked every time.

I worked at a bar in Vancouver, and this was really the best place for scamming. I would meet all kinds of people there. And I wasn't the only scammer on the streets; truth is, there was lots of us, and we got to know each other pretty good. We had this secret game we played on the streets, but it wasn't against each other. Thing is, we actually looked out for one another. But this game was about how to beat one another in the art of scamming. The idea was to see who could pull the best scam. We would sometimes meet up with one another and share our tricks of the trade and see who had the best scams going. It was actually pretty exciting. We never got hung up on who got hurt, and yeah, some people did, but surviving has no feelings. The real game of life was one we were actually playing, and we were just trying to make it to the next day. I became pretty good at it too. I ain't gonna lie. Now, I ain't gonna tell you all my secrets 'cause revealing them might land me in jail, but a few were no-brainers. Besides the scammers, we had hookers and old horny men that would hang around the bar. I was in a good position, 'cause I would get the stories before anyone, and some of them ol' fellas, well, they weren't looking to pay no hookers, and they was just looking for some good company. I was a very good listener and talker. I had a place next door to the bar, but the buildings were joined like one. I worked hard to make money, but it was never enough, and so from time to time, I would invite one of them ol' bastards to my place for some company. Anyway, I would tell them up front that I was not going to screw them, 'cause Stella had good morals and all. Anyways, some of them liked that. They liked that I was into just talking. Sometimes them ol' guys just needed someone to listen to them and that was all I did. They paid me too, but I did feel kind of bad for getting paid when they didn't even get a feel. Some of them were creepy, so those ones I didn't mind pulling a scam job on.

Anyways, the best scam I had was the phone call scam. I had a friend working with me on this one. Her name was Gina. Anyway, Gina lived next door to me, and I would walk pass her door on the way to mine. Sometimes I would stop at her door and knock before going to my place with one of the guys. Mind you, I only did this scam to the creepy old rich guys 'cause I knew they wouldn't miss their money. **I had standards**! Anyways, When Gina would answer her door, I would tell her that her mailbox was full downstairs and that maybe she should go check the mail. That was our signal. I had a phone in my place, and after about an hour of entertaining and being a good listener to the old farts, Gina would call, pretending to be someone else. This is where my love for acting would kick in. Anyways, Gina would say to me that she is sorry to inform me that there has been a terrible accident, and my brother or sister, or auntie, or whoever Gina decided on, was hit by a bus or something like that, andthey were in the hospital in Edmonton. She would tell me the family has been called in. Again, I know this was not a nice thing to do, but man, I needed money like everyone else, and I really didn't want to start selling what my momma gave me. Anyways, I would start crying really hard. The act of crying did get easier for me over time, and sometimes, I'd let the flood gates open. I don't know, maybe during those times, I really was crying for things that had went wrong in the past. But anyways, I would cry and tell whatever old guy that was with me that there was an accident, and my family member was involved, and I had to figure out how to get some money together to get to Edmonton. Usually, the old dudes would bring out their wallets and give me the extra cash on top of the "visitor" fee. This one time, this scam almost backfired on us when this one guy tells me he'd drive me to Edmonton himself. Man, I had a hard time getting out of that one. I'll tell you the story.

Well, like I said, Gina would always make the call, and this one time, she told me my nephew fell off the roller coaster at the West Edmonton Mall, and that he's in bad shape. Anyways, the old man I am "visiting" tells me that he was on his way to Edmonton in a few days but was willing to leave right away to help me out. I was caught in my scam, so I had to think fast. I tell him to go wait for me at the bar, that I had to pack and get ready. By this time, I panic and don't know how to get out of this one, so I tell Gina she has to come with me. On our way down to the bar, we meet up with Daniel, his friend Jimmy Nine-Toes, and Scabs. I tell them my situation, and Jimmy starts to cry, "Oh my son, my son, I need to get to my son."

We all go down to the bar, and we meet the old guy, and I tell him that Gina, Daniel, Jimmy, and Scabs all have to come with me. I tell him that Jimmy is my brother, and that it is his son that is in the accident. I tell him we all have to go. Well, just like that, the old man changes his mind and tells me that something came up and he can't make the trip anymore. He pulls out forty bucks from his wallet and tells me I best take the bus. That was a close one. He leaves the bar quick, and me and my friends cross the street to the next bar and have a few drinks to celebrate the scam. Scamming was like that. It was just a game of survival to those of us that didn't get the top half of the deck with the better laid out "plans" for life.

BUS STATION BUDDIES AND OTHER STRANGERS

Poor Mr. Evans, his face seemed to crinkle a little as I read about my scamming ways. I know he's in there, and I know he hears me. Judy too is starting to believe me when I tell her that his facial expressions seem to change a bit, depending on what kind of mood he might be in. The nurse tells us again not to get our hopes up too much, but I believe in miracles. I had to, 'cause without them, I'd be dead long ago. I'm still here, and there were times I wonder how I made it through, and I guess this is where I convinced myself that my life is a moving miracle. I, for one, wasn't about to give up on Mr. Evans. I believed that one day he would wake up. I was just going to keep believing for something better **'cause losing hope was the best way to walk into a grave.** And I ain't gonna walk Mr. Evans there just yet. Besides, in my time, I meet some crazy people, been to places, and did stuff that could have had me six feet under. I survived some crazy-ass shit, so in my heart of hearts, I believed Mr. Evans could survive this too. I was no quitter, so I wasn't ready to quit on Mr. Evans just yet. Besides, I really needed him now. He was the only one I could really share my stories with, and I knew he wasn't going to judge me. Well, I hope not anyways.

But back to my story.

The "bus ticket to Edmonton" scam was not always a scam; sometimes I really did use the money to take the bus. I never learned to drive, and well, I couldn't afford a car even if I could. The busses and the bus stations were familiar places, and sometimes I would spend days jumping from one bus to another to get from one place to the next. Sometimes, my bus ride was my time to think about how the hell I ended up in places I had no business going to. Like the time I ended up in Toronto.

Anyways, I was living and working in Vancouver, and my boss there tells me that he's opening a new bar in Toronto and asks me one night if I'd be interested in working there. He tells me that I know the business pretty good on the part of not taking crap from the customers, and that I handle them well. I guess it was his way of telling me that I was a good worker and that I was pretty good with the customers. I wasn't mean to them unless I needed to be, and mostly, I was able to ask them to leave nicely without too much trouble most times. I had learned how to talk to people, and I guess my boss liked that in me. I tell him that I'd give it a try. Well, anyway, he tells me that he has some folks already running the place and that they could use my help. He tells me I could pack up, and he'd pay my bus ticket to Toronto. I catch the bus on a Wednesday, and the weird part is that I still remember this. Anyways, I get to Calgary and strike up a conversation with a rather handsome gentleman who was also headed to Toronto. He tells me he lives there, and we get pretty friendly real fast. We chat on the bus all the way to Toronto. When we get there, we are both real tired, and he tells me that I can come crash at his place. At the time, I think it's a great idea and follow him. Well, everything goes real good. We get to his place, and I fall asleep on his couch. When I get up, there are people there, real hippie types. Smelt kind of funny too. So, the guy, he wakes me up and asks me if I want a drink. I figure one can't hurt but tell him that I had to get going soon. He gives me a drink and I swear the asshole put some kind of drug in there 'cause now I think I'm in some sort of flying saucer, and my world is crazy colourful. Anyways, to make a long story short, I end up staying there, high as a kite for a couple crazy days. Weird thing is, time just seemed to stand still and everything was all wonky and all. I still remember going to the bathroom, looking at my pee and thinking there is a rainbow flowing out of my twat. Looking in the mirror was freaky too. I remember trying to wash my face and looking in the mirror. I swear an alien was looking back at me. Everybody's voice sounded so far away, and it was like everything was in slow motion. I tried to sleep it off, but closing my eyes was real scary too. Every now and again, the guy (to this day, I can't remember his name) would give me a drink or something to eat.

I finally snap out of it after a few days, and I tell the guy that I have to leave to go to my new job. The guy calls me a cab, and off I go to check out the new bar only to find out I am fired before I even start. For crying out loud, I guess I was supposed to arrive a week ago, and I was a week late. The bus trip home was a long one. At least the manager had the decency to buy me a ticket back to Vancouver with the promise I work off the ticket once I got back to Vancouver. I felt pretty bad for what went down that time. I am usually pretty good at keeping my word, but once I get distracted and talking, I sometimes lose focus.

Bus stations were a safe place for me when things were getting tough in life, and let me tell you, things weren't always easy. Sometimes, I had no home for short periods of time, and so I would go to the bus station and pretend like I am waiting for someone or waiting to take a bus. I was at a bus station this one time in Edmonton when I met my first real love. Told me his name was Jack. Anyway, I met Jack at the bus station. From the minute I laid eyes on him, I was oh-la-la. I couldn't even look him straight 'cause he was so handsome. He had black hair and had a nice black mustache. I just wanted him to rub that black mustache all over my face.

Anyways, I was sitting at the bus station after leaving Vancouver 'cause my scams were starting to catch up to me, and I had pissed a few people off, so I thought I'd go lay low somewhere else for a while. I took the bus to Edmonton but really had no place to go. I had planned to maybe eventually hitchhike to Chief Meetos. I was just too tired to go any further, so I thought I'd rest at the station for a few hours. I had been sitting there, just minding my own biz, when I spotted Jack sitting in a seat in the next row over. He looked tired and looked like he needed someone to talk to. Plus, he was so good-looking. Anyway, I decided to do my "Stella move." I get up and walk towards him. As I'm walking, I'm pretending to be digging in my purse for something, even though all I had was a half-eaten sandwich, half a pack of smokes, my comb, and my change purse. So, I am walking, digging away, and right when I get close, I pretend I lose direction and walk right into his legs. I pretend to laugh and say, "Oh, I'm sorry," throwing my hair to the side.

The chair next to him is empty, so I sit and keep looking in my purse. Finally, I say out loud, "Shit, I wonder where I put my keys."

I sit there and act all confused and everything, and finally, Jack says, "Yeah, I hate it when I lose my keys too."

So, he and I start talking, and turns out he know Donna, my long-lost buddy from Chief Meetos. He tells me he lives close to Waldrom, just about an hour out of Edmonton. Tells me he's waiting for his daughter to get off the bus from Calgary, but the bus is running late. So, I sit there with him, talking. Anyways, to make a long story short, his daughter didn't get off the bus that day, but Jack, he ain't going home empty handed either and takes me home instead.

I ended up living with Jack for over a year. Jack had a small farm-like place close to Waldrom. Jack's house was small, but it was better than what I had been living in. I kept it clean and followed the only rule he had for me, which was never to go to the big barn he had out in the field area. It seemed that Jack had some things he didn't want me to know about, but it was none of my business, so I don't ask. I was just happy I had a roof over my head, food to eat, the odd beer when I wanted one, and a damn good-looking man to crawl into bed with every night. Jack worked in town, but I never asked what he did. He gave me money when I needed it and bought me clothes. I was happy just having someone to love, and for someone to love me. We really did fall in love, me and Jack. I even met his daughter a few times, and she came up to stay with us that first Christmas I was with Jack. For the first time in my life, I really felt I had a family, or at least close to one anyways. Things were going good, but then one day, the cops show up asking me questions about Jack. I tell them I don't know nothing, which was the truth 'cause I didn't make it a point to snoop in all Jack's business. Jack was at work that day, and they asked me where Jack is. I tell the cop that Jack is at work. They ask me where exactly Jack worked, and I tell them that he works in town, just didn't know where. When Jack came home that night, I tell him the cops came by, and he gets all scared. I ask him why he's acting all weird, and he asks me what I told them. I tell him, "I know nothing, so I tell them nothing."

Jack, well—that evening, he hit the bottle real hard and paced the house all hours of the night. When he finally got to bed, I hear vehicles pulling up outside, so I look out the window. Next thing I know, the cops are busting the door down, and me and

Jack are on the floor, handcuffed. The cops are now asking me questions I can't answer. Jack's still drunk and decides he's going to try to make a run for it. I'm yelling at him to settle down, but as I am yelling, Jack makes his move to the stairs. The officer chases him up. He reaches up to grab Jack, but Jack turns around and kicks the officer right in the face. At that moment, everything seems to freeze in time. My heart sinks, 'cause I know that everything Jack and I had going just got kicked out the door. There is blood everywhere, and Jack knows he's beat, so he climbs back down the stairs, lays on the floor, and waits for his arrest. The other cop takes him and throws him in the wagon. The cop leaves me inside, handcuffed, then comes back and asks where Jack store all the goods. I tell him I have no idea what he's talking about. Finally, after about a half-hour or so, one cop comes in and tells the other one that he found all the goods in the barn out back. Jack and I are both taken to the station and charged for theft over five thousand dollars. By this time, I am freaking out wondering what the hell Jack got into, and no one is talking. They throw me in the cells with no chance to talk.

I go in the cell, yelling at the guard, telling him I don't know anything. He tells me to save it for the judge, and to enjoy my stay. I look around the cell and find I am in company with a three-hundred-pound-plus chick. She smiles at me and tells me everything is going to be ok. I smile back and say nothing. I am tired and scared wondering what is going to happen to me. I still did not have any clue what kind of shit Jack was into, and I was glad I didn't know. At least when I made my plea with the judge, I didn't have to try to act innocent this time, 'cause I really was. Anyway, the chick, she must notice I am freaking out and asks me if I want to cuddle with her. I tell her to fuck off and to leave me alone. She warns me to sleep with one eye open, and suddenly I am not so tired. I still remember fighting off sleep in the wee hours of morning, praying Little Lotta didn't try to come spoon me.

The next morning, they take me to a judge where I am asked for my full name. The judge looks at me and tells the court helper to run my name in the system. The court helper leaves then comes back in a few minutes, and bam, I was caught on the old assault charge from that bar incident so long ago. Anyway, the judge tells me they are going to keep me in for the assault charge, and I will also be charged for theft. At this point, my TV watching kicks in, and I ask for a lawyer.

I get assigned a free lawyer, who bargains me out on the assault charges, and I get thirty days in jail. I come clean with my lawyer and plea that I have no idea about the theft I am being accused of. I ask to speak with Jack. I tell my lawyer that Jack will clear everything up 'cause at that point I still have no idea what they think I stole. My lawyer finally tells me that I am being charged for stealing farm equipment parts. I just couldn't believe it. What the hell would I do with farm equipment parts? Anyway, to make a long story short, I was found innocent, and Jack ended up in jail for eighteen months.

Jail was not as bad as I thought it was going to be. Besides the in-house affairs that went on with the ladies, I kept out of their business, and they left me alone too. The food was not the greatest, but shit, I ain't going to complain, long as it was it was not me cooking or doing the dishes. Some of the ladies in there were scary, but I learn real fast to stay low and out of sight. I told myself, "Stella, just do your time and get the hell out." And so, I did.

I had one friend. Corrina was her name. One day, I ask Corrina what she was in for, and she tells me the story of shoving a carrot up an old guy's ass. As soon as she say "carrot," my mind does a fast track to my first. Anyways, my guess was that it was a pretty big carrot 'cause she do some real damage up in there. Corrina, she has a good sense of humor, so I ask her if the guy's name was Bugs. We laugh a bit, and she continues to tell me the story. Corrina was beautiful. And when I mean beautiful, I don't mean slutty beautiful but brown skin beautiful. She had this black hair that was so thick and long. Even if she didn't shower, her hair still looked shiny. She had big, beautiful dark brown eyes, and her skin was smooth brown. I've heard some inmates refer to her as Pocahontas. But I wasn't going to call her that 'cause the real story about Pocahontas is not one anyone should be pretending is all romantic. I mean, I bet the girl they call Pocahontas was real beautiful and all, but the fucked up shit that happened to her was not good. I had heard the story and heard she was just a kid. And I guess if it were my daughter, I wouldn't want people talking that rape and murder is something romantic. So, I just call her "Corrina" to respect the family of the girl they did call Pocahontas.

Anyways, this one night, Corrina is at the bar with her friends, and she meets this guy. She tells me that he looked friendly enough, and they got to drinking and talking and talking and drinking some more. She said she had no plans to go home with him, 'cause he's just a bit too old for her, but she liked the company and attention he gave her. Anyway, she says she didn't remember much of what happened next, but she remembers waking up on cold ground. She said she looks around and sees a garden or something like that. She recalled not being able to breathe 'cause the old man was on top of her and was trying to put his penis into her. She said she felt cold and believed that it must have been the cold air that brought her to her senses. He was heavy, but somehow, she manages to push him off. She manages to get up and tries to run away, but he chases her. There is a greenhouse nearby—you know, one of them plastic covered houses for growing plants—so she runs in there looking for something to fight him off with. She finds a tub laying on the floor filled with vegetables, so she grabs a carrot from the pile. Just as she grabs the carrot, the old man runs in and corners her. He grabs her and throws her back on the ground. As she is falling, she manages to gain her strength back and grabs on to the ledge of a nearby table and gets her balance back. He proceeds to attack her, but now she is fighting for her life, so she pushed him away from her as hard as she could. She says she managed to get out from his grip and pushed him, so he falls on the floor with his ass facing her. Not knowing how long he will stay down, and with the carrot still in her hand, she stabs the carrot right into his ass. She said she leaves him there, bleeding, finds his truck, and steals it to escape. She tells me she run out of gas about twenty miles out and falls asleep in the truck. She said she wakes up to the cops telling her to come out. Anyway, she gets charged for the assault, but they drop the charges on the truck theft. The old man walks, 'cause now he's the victim. Even though he was the one that tried to rape her. **He was white; she was a brown skin. And that is just how it is.**

Anyway, Corrine asks me why I call us Indian girls "brown skins." Told her I didn't like the word "Indian" too much 'cause I had learned in school how Columbus got lost and thought he landed his boat in India. I also learned that he was a pretty sick fucker and did some sick shit to us, so I didn't like the name much. I really didn't know what other word to use either, so I use "brown skin."

Anyways, Corrina was my experimental stage of making out with a woman. At that point, I wasn't sure if I was into women but knew that I was just really lonely and needed someone to comfort me. I was missing Jack too, but I knew that was over. So, Corrina and I got together that one evening. I won't say it was bad, but it really was not my cup of tea either. And like I said, I was lonely. The whole experience had me thinking about different types of relationships. I got along pretty good with Corrina, and if I was into ladies, I am sure I would have been happy with her. I guess living all over the place and meeting all kinds of people, I never really thought about who was who. I just think of people as either being good or bad.

I haven't thought about Corrina in a long time. Thinking back on my life is like watching some kind of crazy movie. Hearing myself read my story seems kind of weird too. It doesn't seem like it's real. It seems like so long ago, like a dream that happened. I know it's not a dream; it really did happen, but some days it is like I am just waking up from a crazy dream and the life in that dream is not real. Not really sure how to explain it, but sometimes that is just how I feel. When I get lost in those times, I look down at Mr. Evans and wonder if he dreams or if he feels like he is living in a dream. Maybe he is, and his dream world is less crazy than this place.

It is nice to read my stories to Mr. Evans. It feels like some stuff is coming off my chest, and I forget the life I had sometimes. As I read to him and share the crazy shit I done, even I surprise me. I sometimes can't believe that I lived through some of this. So, in a sense, reading to him is like being at confession or something. Not that everything I did was bad and needs forgiving, but it was nice to hear my own words. Everything seems so calm now—my life, I mean. I don't worry about not having a place to crash. I have my own bed. Little things like that, well, they seem insignificant to some, but to me, it's a big deal. I like having quiet in my life. Well, for now anyways. I am a Coyote. That's the thing about coyotes; they make their family with whoever is around them. Maybe that is how I survived so long.

I came to work this morning and found Mrs. Evans crying by Mr. Evans bed. I quickly get to the bed, thinking the worst has happened. I put my hand on Judy's shoulder and ask her if everything is ok. She looks up at me, big tears falling, and tells how she misses him. She tells me she feels bad that she leaves him all day for me to look after. I tell her I don't mind. I felt so sorry for her. I tell her that I read to him about the stuff I am writing, and sometimes it seems like his face wants to break out in a smile. I tell her that he's still in there fighting to get his strength back so he can wake up. Judy tells me to go home for the day and that she's going to take a day off. I ask her if I can stay, 'cause I really had some writing fuel. That's when Judy brings out this box and hands me the best gift ever. She bought me a computer I can carry around and a bag to put it in. I also cry. No one ever done anything this nice for me in a long time. Well, Judy and I spend a few hours that morning setting up my laptop. I guess that's what it's called: a laptop. Now I can write when I'm at home. It was like having a birthday today. That night I go home, but on my way, I buy myself a little cake and pretend that it is my birthday, and that Judy and Mr. Evans are my parents. **It is the best feeling to feel loved.**

ONE-NIGHT LOVE AFFAIRS AND OTHER STUFF

I am not really sure if I even want to write about these times, but I guess it can't hurt now. Those days are gone, and I can't undo what I already done. In my early years, when I got into the drinking, I was a little crazier some times more than others. I guess I was in my prime. No one ever told me about how to have a relationship with a man, and it seemed the crowds I was hanging around with was just screwing everyone and each other. No one seemed to have rules about that stuff, and it was all just normal to everyone around. Like the friends I was hanging around with, I had some crazy love flings too. Some of them I fell in love with when I was drunk, only to wake up sober and fall out of love just as fast. I want to share a few of those stories.

There was this one night club in Vancouver called Nite Grooves. Anyway, when I wasn't working my bar, some friends of mine would take me there. I was young and looking for fun. Nite

Grooves brought out the craziness in all of us. Anyway, this one time, we decided to get out for some dancing and having a good time. It was nothing unusual, just some drinking and dancing. Anyways, I met this guy. His name, I think, was Art, or Bob. Something like that; I don't really remember. I will just call him Art. Anyway, I had noticed him other times when I was at the bar, just standing around, not really drinking, not really dancing either. A couple of those times, as I would walk to the bathroom, he'd be leaning up against a wall. Real mysterious. Anyways, on a couple of those times, I would just walk by and say hi. I never asked him to dance. Nothing—just a hello. Anyway, this one night, he comes to talk to me just as the bar is closing and ask me where we are going. I tell him that my friends and I are going to an afterparty at some address I didn't recognize. But this guy was walking around the bar handing out the address. I ask him if he wants to tag along, and he says, "Sure."

So, we get outside pile into someone's car when Art says he has a car too, and if anyone is sober enough, we can separate the group and take both cars. We do this, and I decide to ride in Art's car with a few of my buddies. My one friend, Carl, tells us that a few blocks down, one of the bars is still open, and he wants to go buy some off sale. We tell him we have enough, but he insists on going anyway, and so our driver does a detour for him. Carl tells us to wait for him in the car, and so we park on the other side of the road. People are just piling out of the bar as we get there. Carl leaves and says he will be right back. We sit in the car waiting with the radio going, listening to some great tunes. A few minutes later, I spot Carl running towards the car like someone is chasing him. He jumps in the car and tells the driver to hurry up and just drive. The driver, well, he panics, and drives off real fast asking Carl what the hell is going on. Carl is laughing now and gives directions to the driver to go to an address that is close by. The driver asks him again what the hell is going on, and Carl pulls out this jar from under his jacket. The jar is full of change and a few five-dollar bills. Damn idiot stole the tip jar from the last bar and now wanted to go buy a couple joints. The driver is pissed off 'cause now he's the driver of a getaway car in a robbery. He tells Carl he's an asshole and stops the car. They argue for a bit, and Carl tells him if they get caught, he would take the heat for it all. Anyways, we get back on track with the night decide to go find the afterparty. We show up at the address, but there are no cars around. We double check the address, and yup, we have the right one. It seemed an odd place for a party, as the neighborhood was nice and all, but we decide to go and ring the doorbell anyways. The next thing we know, some guy comes charging out the door screaming and yelling at us to get the fuck off his property or he's calling the cops next time someone rings his doorbell. We jump back in the car and peel away again for the second time in the night. What the hell anyways? Well, after we realize there is no party there, we head back to my little place and sit around for a few drinks. The driver—still can't remember his name—he lives a few blocks east, so he leaves shortly after having a few beers.

Now I am stuck with Carl and Art and kind of hoping that Carl would catch a cab back to his place so I can make the move on Art. Anyway, we get back to my place and I put on some mood type music on my eight-track player as a way to drop hints that I am interested in this mystery man I've brought home. The three of us get to drinking some more, and soon enough, Carl is passed out on the couch. I am feeling no pain at this point, so I tell Art that I am going to bed and he's free to join me. He tells me that he'll just head out and catch a cab, and he has me wondering what the heck I did for him to show no interest. Again, like I say, I am feeling no pain, so I just ask him what's up with him, and he tells me that I am too young for him. Of course, this sounds weird to me 'cause it looka like I am older than him.

I laugh and ask him how old he is, and he tell me. He's two years younger than me, so I ask why he say I'm too young when I am older than him. He tells me he's into much older women, like ones in their mid-forties to early fifties. I chuckle at him and tell him goodnight, then close the door as he leaves. I never did see him again. I asked about him a few times and heard that he found himself a sugar momma and moved to Kamloops.

Booze, sex, and common sense don't go together for some people, and at times, I was one of them people. Anyways, when I drink, I like to chew gum, and not just any gum, but that big pink chewy kind. Anyways, this one time I was on shift when this guy asks me if there are any hookers in the bar. I point to a few of them, but he tells me they are all ugly. I tell him the hotel rooms have lights; just shut them off, and he wouldn't notice.

He just laughs and says, "What about you?"

I say, "What about me?"

Then he asks, "Ever have sex for money?"

I tell him that I did no such thing, that if I was hooking, then I wouldn't be working this bar.

Anyway, he says, "What if I offered you five hundred dollars for an hour?"

I am thinking, "Wow, five hundred dollars for an hour."

The guy, well, he was not too hard on the eyes, and I have a room close by, so it would be easy. I tell him I'd give it a shot 'cause five hundred bucks is five hundred bucks, so I tell him to wait until the bar closes. Anyway, the last hour of work, I am real nervous and start sneaking drinks. By the time I'm done my shift, I am feeling pretty good. I tell the guy to come with me to my room, and when we get in, I pound back a few more rye and cokes. Except there is more rye than there is coke. I am pretty drunk now and decide I hate my breath and pop in some gum. Anyways, I tell the guy to pay up first, acting like I am a pro at this. While he's shelling out his cash, I am praying he's not a killer or some sex freak, promising myself I would do this just once but never again. We crawl into bed, and the guy tells me that he's married, and I'm like, "What the hell?"

He continues and tells me that it is not considered cheating if I just give him a blow job. I am pretty drunk, and the guy already paid me my money, so I think, "What the hell, may as well give it a shot."

So, I go down there, gum still in my mouth, and proceed to do my business when I realize my gum has fallen out of my mouth and is now stuck on his hair. Down there. I tried my best to keep doing a good "job" all while trying to pick the gum out. In the end, I had to tell the guy he has gum stuck all over his pubic hair and his balls. We end our night with him pissed off and having to go home to his wife with half of his hair shaved off. The next morning, I wake up with bits and pieces of the night only to be reminded of what went down when I walk into my bathroom and see there is pubic hair all over the place. The only good thing that came out of the whole thing is that I ended up with five hundred dollars. I guess I pissed off the guy so much, he forgot to ask me back for his money. Thinking back, I probably should have charged him for the haircut.

Another crazy story: this one time, I was out in Edmonton when I met this guy at a bar. Anyway, he tells me that he wants to have crazy, wild sex with me, so I tell him to take me back to his place. Again, I was under the influence and not thinking straight. I would never in a million years tell others to do the things I did 'cause I was living without rules, and in this day and age, that shit is just scary. Anyways, he tells me that he still lives with his parents, but that we should go for a drive. Of course, being in the state that I was in, I was not really thinking. I realize now there were so many bad things that could have happened during those times. Anyways, I am lucky nothing bad did happen, but if I were to do it again, I wouldn't. So anyways, I tell the guy that we should take a drive, and we end up on some country road. There is no traffic where he takes me, and we proceed to do the deed. Anyways, things get real heavy real quick. By this time, it is daylight out 'cause its summer. I am not sure how to position myself, so the guy tells me to open the window of his car and just hang out. My pants are off, but I still have my shirt on. I proceed to do what he asks, and now half of my body is hanging out the car. He proceeds to hump me, and as he gets going, a car is approaching. Now I didn't want to stop the rhythm, so I just stay hanging out the car window. The car slows down as it is passing, and I am praying they don't stop. So here I am, trying hard to smile at the old couple that has slowed to see what is going on. I manage to wave them through, breaking out a smile as I do. Anyway, it was a tense situation that time. Not to mention embarrassing.

It's hard writing about this secret stuff in my life, so I decide not to tell Mr. Evans all the stories. I figured it'd be wrong to share this stuff with a man in a coma, and I figure that later when he wakes up, he can read all about my Stella ways. Mrs. Evans asked me how my writing is coming, and I tell her how thankful I am for everything she done to make me feel good enough about myself to write. No one ever made me feel good like that. Really feels like I can do something with my life for the first time. I remember someone once telling me that **it's better to live knowing you are going to leave something people will remember you by rather than to leave a blank slate.** I know I ain't no celebrity, and no one really knows my name, but **the least I can do for this world is leave a damn good story.**

RANDOM THOUGHTS

Sometimes, my mind just wanders to all them memories I have stored inside my head. I think about the places I ended up, the people I met, and the things I done. Sometimes, those memories feel like I am watching a TV show. Sometimes, I just laugh to myself, but sometimes, I cry too 'cause not everything I seen was good. Not everything I done was good too. I am lucky I met the Evans family; they sure slowed me down to make me think about life. I think about them. How they trust in someone like me. An old Coyote like me. I suit my name too.

You ask a person what animal they want to be when they die and many will say they want to be an eagle or a wolf or a hummingbird, and some even say a cat. Them crazy ones, they say they want to be a unicorn. Me, I'm a Coyote to the end. No one ever says they want to be a pesky coyote. Coyotes are sneaky, and their fur is not the nicest. And they got them sneaky eyes saying they just want to get into mischief. In a way, I was kind of like that, except I didn't go looking for trouble; trouble just seemed to find me. I seem to always end up with people that did crazy things too. Sometimes I just seem to be at the wrong place at the wrong time, sometimes even with the wrong people. But it toughened me up, and I can survive pretty much anything. I mean, look at me, living with these rich white folks that took me in like a stray cat off the streets. That is luck, I tell ya. It's the Coyote way. **I am my own name**.

Sometimes I think I am the crazy one around here until I meet others that are crazier. And some that are just real weird. Some people have some crazy habits too. I remember this one time, I was in Calgary for a few days. Well, I think I might have been stuck there or something. Anyways, one thing I have going for me is I am pretty friendly and get along with anyone who will talk to me. Well, when I was in Calgary, and I don't even remember how I got there, I ended up at this house, partying. Anyways, the party, it gets out of hand, and the cops show up and bust things up. Everyone is told to get out. No one listens to the cops, and everyone keeps going. Then, this one guy gets crazy and grabs one of them fire things they use to put fires out and starts spraying that crap all over the place. Now people are scrambling to get the hell out. The cops are freaking out trying to tackle the guy while people are tripping on each other trying to get outside. Man, that was one crazy night. Anyways, I make it outside, but I'm wondering now where I'm going to go, 'cause my pass out spot has just been taken from me. Anyways, there is this lady there that I had been talking and drinking with, and she somehow finds me in the crowd and tells me I can go camp at her house for the night. I'm pretty happy I'll have a place to sleep, so I tell her I'll go with her.

We walk for what seems like hours before getting to her house, and by the time we get to her place, I am as sober as a judge. I ask her if she has anything to drink, and she say she has plenty. We get into her house, and to this day, I still can't remember her name. But anyways, we get into her house, and holy shit, I almost died. There was crap all over the place, boxes on boxes. Junk.

"Holy shit," I'm thinking to myself, "where the hell am I supposed to sleep in this mess?"

I don't say nothing to the lady, 'cause now I think she might kill me, and nobody will ever find my body in her house. But I can't sleep in her mess either. The smell was pretty bad too, and I was wondering if maybe there really were dead things in the house. Anyways, she tells me to come in and make myself at home. And in my mind, I start to laugh 'cause I have no real home, and if I did, it wouldn't be at a junk yard. I ask her where the bathroom is, and she points to a door that is painted pink and has flowers glued on it. It looked like she at least was trying to make her house nice, but who the hell glues dried up flowers on their doors? But anyways, I go to the bathroom, and holy shit, the tub is full of shampoo bottles. So, I take one, and it's empty, and I'm wondering now how she clean herself. Just over the bathtub is a window, and I'm measuring it up to see if I can fit through there. I decide to give it a try and manage to open the window. I stand on the tub and manage to jump to the open window ledge. There is only one problem. I look down, and there is a bit of a drop into some kind of bush and nothing to hang on to. I decide to dive into the bush, 'cause I don't want to take my chances with the crazy junk lady. I land face first into the bush. I remember hurting real bad, but nothing was broken. I manage to get myself out of the bush, scratches and all. I leave her yard through the back alley. I still remember finding an open shed a few houses down and sleeping in there for a few hours. Somehow, I made it back to Vancouver hitchhiking all the way. Man, I sure done some crazy things.

When a person live like I do, fights are bound to happen. The street life is hard, and if anyone out there thinks it's easy on the people that hang out there, they best think again. Trust me, it ain't no easy life. The streets are mean. Rough. Tough. I had to be tough to survive this life, and walking away from a fight was something I didn't do. I couldn't afford to be known as the chicken on the street. Sometimes, the fights I got into had some meaning, had a purpose, but other times, the fight was just stupid. I want to share a story about a crazy fight I got into this one time.

Anyway, I had a friend who was a street girl. When I say street girl, I mean she was a hooker. I really don't like that word 'cause the girls I meet that sell for sex, well they is human just the same as the girl who doesn't. These girls, they get a bad reputation because of what they do, but I will tell you some truth about this. Yeah, many are brown skins working to survive, but many of their johns are white men with wives and children. Maybe many won't like that truth but that's exactly what it is. I met lots of the girls in the bar I work at and seen that they were just trying to survive like I was. I didn't judge them. Most of them were pretty nice, and some of them became my good friends. I felt safe when I was with the girls. No one messed with them. They were tough as nails. Anyway, one of my buddies. Shit, I can't seem to remember her name right now, but I still remember what she looked like. She had this long, thick black hair that hung down her back. She wasn't very tall, but she was built stocky. She had these big brown eyes, and just under one of them was this scar that connected to her eye brow. I remember her this way 'cause this was how we started talking that day she walked into my bar. She told me that some john tried to cut her up, and as he swung his knife at her, she went down to duck. He managed to clip her across the face, just beside her eye as she was turning down. Anyways, she worked the street my bar was on. Sometimes, when I wasn't working, I would leave my room where I lived and would go for a walk. I would see the crazy outside world in the middle of the day—things I mostly heard about in the bar. There were benches spaced apart along the street, usually two to a street. The girls had their own special benches, and Lydia—that was her name—had her own bench. When Lydia was on her bench, people who knew the rules of the streets knew not to sit there. It was her bench. The streets were kind of crazy like that. Those that hung out on the street knew the rules, and if a person didn't know the rules, things could get crazy real fast. Once in a while, there would be a situation. I was pleased that although I wasn't a street girl, I knew the rules—the ins and outs of how things went down.

Lots of times, the girls took the hit for the streets being a "bad place." But if it wasn't for the guys that came to buy sex, no one would be in business. Well, this one time, this guy I know, Jake, comes into the bar in the middle of the afternoon. I wasn't working that day but had gone down to sit and have a quiet drink. Anyways, I am sitting there when Jake walks in, and he's half cut and looking for someone to talk to, so he plops his fat ass next to where I am sitting. We start chatting when Jake tells me he's real horny and looking for some loving. I tell him he's barking up the wrong tree 'cause I ain't like that. So, he tells me that he would pay me a finder's fee if I found him a decent-looking afternoon friend he could spend a few hours with. Now, I was no pimp, but I wasn't going to shy away from making a quick buck either. Opportunity was opportunity. I tell him I will help him out. I tell Jake that maybe he and I should go for a walk downtown to see who was out and about. Of course, before we leave the bar, I tell Jake that I want half of my finder's fee up front. I also tell him to stay quiet and let me talk 'cause he's drunk and not familiar with the rules out on the street. Jake nods, and we agree on a finder's fee of twenty bucks. Jake gives me ten off the bat, and we start walking.

Anyways, Jake and I don't get too far when I notice Lydia at her bench. She's not alone though, and I notice her sitting with another lady—kind of manly looking. I tell Jake I know the lady sitting on the bench, and that she's a working girl. He looks over to the bench and tells me he likes what he sees and wants an introduction. I tell him to say nothing when we get there, and I would do all the talking, but you got to remember, Jake is drunk and horny. Anyway, we walk up to Lydia and her friend, and I ask her how she's doing. She tells me she's good and introduces me to her friend Roxy. I tell Lydia that I want to talk to her alone, 'cause I don't know what the deal is with Roxy. Lydia and I walk away from the bench, leaving Jake there. I tell him to stay put, and to stay quiet. Lydia and I walk a little ways away, when I hear a racket, and from the corner of my eye, I see Jake getting his ass kicked by Roxy. Lydia and I run up to the two to see what the hell is going on. Jake is on the ground, and Roxy on top pounding him. I grab Roxy from behind to help out my friend but accidently rip her wig off. Holy shit, Roxy was a guy dressed up as a lady. Somehow, I sensed something, but I don't like to judge people. Anyways, Lydia jumps in and holds Roxy down, but by this point the only thing I could do was save Jake, so I grab him and we high tail it back to the bar. Jake is bleeding by the mouth, and his shirt is all ripped up. When we're in the clear, I ask him what the hell happened with Roxy, and he tells me that he thought Roxy was pretty sexy and thought that was the girl I was trying to set him up with. I guess Jake told Roxy that he wouldn't mind taking a peek at what was under the skirt and that was when all hell broke loose. Roxy was no hooker, and I guess Jake being a drunk horny ass really insulted her. Anyways, Lydia and I had a good laugh about that way later. And Jake, well, he paid to bang Lydia a week later, after the big cut on his lip healed.

One thing about my job and taking the time to listen to people talk is the stuff they are willing to tell me. It had been a slow day at the bar when a young man came in. He looked like he just lost his best friend, so I be extra nice to him on a count that I didn't want to add more shit to his plate. He sits alone, and I serve about four beers before the young chap start talking. And I mean *talking*, like I was one of them catholic confession booths or something. Not that I ever went into one of them things, but I knew about them. Anyways, this kid, he was young, maybe twenty-five or something. Anyways, I go drop off the fourth beer when I notice tears in his eyes, so I sit down to ask him if he needs to talk or something. I regret doing that. This story is wacky. Anyways, the kid, he just starts spilling his guts and going on about how he is shy and all, and so finding a girlfriend has always been hard. I go to tell him that I can help with some advice when he starts to cry and says it's all over. Now, I have no clue what the kid is talking about, and part of me is thinking, "Why the hell did I open my big mouth 'cause now I am dealing with a crier."

The kid just starts sobbing and saying his mom kick him out of the house, and he have no place to go. I didn't want to pry, 'cause most stuff is just none of my business, but he just keeps pouring his guts out on how his mom caught him with his blow-up doll. Now, I try hard not to judge people, and as far as I'm concerned, better him with a blow-up than him going out and getting himself into worse trouble, so I tell him maybe his mom was being too hard on him and maybe he best go home and try explain that having a blow-up was no crime. Then the kid, in between sobs, says that he and his blow-up were in his mom's room, and he had put his mom's clothes on the blow-up. He was just about to have his way with the blow-up when his mom walked in and caught him. Man, I met some different people there.

Another story I heard in the bar this one time was about this guy who, and I shit you not, was some kind of burglar or thief. Anyways, he come into the bar this one time; he'd just gotten out after doing a six-month stint. I never asked what they do time for, but this guy struck me as being a bit of an odd ball when he asked me if he can buy my panties off me. At first, I thought the fucker was joking, but when I laughed, he looked me straight in the eye and said he'll pay twenty bucks. I tell him he can run to the department store and grab a few for less than twenty. Then, he says he like the smell. I am thinking to myself, "This guy is sick," but then again, twenty bucks is twenty bucks. Yeah, there are all kinds of people out there. Some have them weird type fetishes, but I learned fast that each to his own, and as long as they stay away from my business, we will get along fine.

FAMILY CONNECTIONS

I think I talked about Gina already, but I got another story about her and me. Anyway, pulling scams together can bring people closer. Wel,l at least, this is what happened to me and Gina. Living close together, drinking together, and sharing our deepest secrets over the years brought me and Gina closer until we became good friends. Every time I needed help, Gina was one sister I could always could on. So, when Gina needed someone to be there for her, I was her girl. This one time, Gina really needed a friend, so I had to be there for her.

We were sitting in the bar one day when a cop walks in and comes to where me and Gina are sitting. The cops were always stopping by, so it was no big deal when one walked in. They were always checking things out 'cause our area was a bit rough at times. What I didn't expect was the cop to come talk to us. Well, to talk to Gina—not really me. Anyways, the cop comes up and asks if Gina's full name was Gina Mary Bishop. Gina, a bit nervous, tells the cop that it was her name and asks why he need to know. The cop then asks Gina to go with him to his cop car 'cause he needs to talk to her in private. Now that get Gina real nervous, but she goes anyways. She leaves for about twenty minutes, then comes back real quiet. I ask her why the cop needed to see her, and she tells me that her name came up back home. I didn't know what the hell she was talking about, so I ask her to explain.

Anyways, she tells me that her sister Joan passed away a month ago, and Gina was the only living family she had left. I guess Joan had a trailer she owned, and now they were looking for the next of kin to look after her affairs. Gina was the name that had been put on Joan's papers for next of kin. They just had a hard time tracking Gina down, but now that they did, she had to go back home to deal with Joan's stuff. Me, being the good friend, and not knowing where "home" was for Gina, tell her I would go with her. After I offer, she tells me that she has to go back to Ontario. I regretted offering at that moment, but figured I said I would go and couldn't back out. I ask my boss for a week off so that I could go with Gina to Ontario. Gina and I decide we would take the bus up to Saskatchewan, then hitchhike through Saskatchewan and Manitoba to save a few bucks. We didn't have a pile of cash with us, but Gina, she keeps talking about the money she was going to get from the trailer that Joan left for her to sell. I didn't worry too much after that. I knew Gina would get us home.

We left on a bus early Monday, and we figured we'd be back by Sunday the latest. Goes to show how much Gina and me knew about selling trailers. Anyways, to make a long story short, it ends up taking us four days to get to Dryden. When we arrive in Dryden, we hitchhike the rest of the way to Gina's home-town of Stockcliff. Gina tells me she had friends that live in the trailer park and says we would look them up for a place to crash. We walk about two miles to the park, and man, what a fucking dump. I mean, I hate to say anything bad about folks, but it was bad. Anyways, we walk up to a trailer that Gina says her friends Maggie and Clint live in. She takes a chance in figuring they still live there 'cause hardly anyone's left in this trailer park. We find the trailer, so I hang back while Gina goes and knocks on the door. A lady answers, and sure as shit, it's that Maggie woman that Gina was talking about. She tells us to come in and tells Gina how sorry she is about Joan's dying, then says she still can't believe that Joan die how she did. At this point, Gina had no idea how her sister died, so she asks Maggie. Maggie tells the story of how Joan drank too much Alberto hair spray and die from poison. She kind of chuckled a bit while telling the story, which I thought was pretty rude, but anyways, she goes on to tell us the rest. She says she, Joan, and a few others were hard up for some drinks, so Clint tells them that they should try hairspray 'cause he heard that people can get drunk on it. Anyways, Joan and another fella go down to the local store and steal some Alberto hairspray. At this point, I am wondering why she insists onsaying, "Alberto hairspray," 'cause she was just stressing the word a bit too much for her story. But anyways, she goes to say they was all drinking and mixing the hairspray with water to wash it down, when Joan falls over. She says that Clint jumps up to try help her, but she hit her head pretty hard on a rock 'cause they are sitting outside when all this happens. Anyways, guess there was blood all over, and ol' Joan just lay there, not saying nothing to no one and not moving either, so they figure they should call for some help. They call for an ambulance, and when the ambulance gets there, Joan is already gone. The cops show up later that night to get the story from them on what happened, and all Clint keep saying is, "Alberto killed her, Alberto killed her."

Next thing, Maggie is laughing, saying that the cop wants a description of Alberto, asking everyone if they knew who this Alberto is. Finally, Maggie, she says she set the cop straight and tells him, "Alberto hairspray, you big dummy."

Guess the cop thought Alberto was some guy. I wanted to laugh at the story, but it's about Gina's sister, so I stay quiet to see what Gina is gonna do. She looked like she wanted to cry, but then starts to laugh. Gina looks at me and says, "If anyone ever asks how my sis died, we tell them Alberto, a crazy guy, killed her. No one needs to know the whole truth."

I just giggle and tell her, "No problem."

Anyway, the last part of the story Maggie tells us is that Joan had no family to claim the body, so the funeral home cremated her, and now it was up to Gina to go pick up the ashes. Maggie says the funeral home is small, so they had no space to keep the body, and just in case no one came for her remains, they creamated her. Anyways, Gina didn't know this part either but says that before we leave, we will make sure that Joan gets a proper service. So, now we are not just dealing with a trailer to sell but have to organize a funeral too. At that point, I'm not sure what I signed myself up for, but because Gina is like a sister, I decide I will support her as much as I could.

We camp that night at Maggie and Clint's place. We spent the evening drinking beers, me listen to them tell stories. Seemed like Gina had a crazy life here. I guess I see why she ended up leaving. Only thing she had that I ain't got is family. I mean, I do have family, but not like these people here, the ones Gina grew up with. The kind a person gets good childhood memories with. I wish I had that sometimes, but I guess it was not part of that "plan" I talked about earlier. We stayed up real late and talked about the service we have to give Joan so that folks can say their last goodbye and stuff. Gina decides to have the service the next night 'cause she has lots to deal with in selling the trailer and all.

The next morning, I get up with a kinked neck from sleeping on the love seat, while Gina sleep on the couch. I wake up to people laughing and find Gina and Maggie having coffee. When I get up, Gina tells me it's time for us to go to the trailer where her sister lived. Luckily, Maggie has a spare key, so we walk to the trailer from Maggie's place. I still remember it took us about twenty minutes 'cause Gina was walking slow. We walk past a bunch of trailers, some of them looking like no one lived in them no more. Some had smashed out windows, and some had boards covering the windows and door. Gina, she keeps walking slow, and it seemed that as we went, her stride got somewhat slower. I felt bad for my friend; I don't think she really wanted to visit the trailer, but it was something she had to do. It was the right thing to do. Anyways, as we were walking, I start thinking about my own family. Our walk was mostly silent, so I had time for some thinking. Mostly, I thought about my brothers and my sister Connie. I wondered how they were doing, wondered if they were still living. If they did die, my only hope was that they were surrounded by people that love them. I'm not really sure how it will be for me when I die. I wonder if all these people around me that call themselves friends and family will really be there. I guess it won't really matter 'cause I'll be gone anyways. But still, I couldn't help but to think about it.

As we approached the trailer, Gina stopped and pointed it out to me.

"This is the one," she said. There were tears in her eyes, something I hadn't seen much of in our trip out here. **I guess even the tough ones had tears built up somewhere**. The trailer was an ugly green colour. It sat lonely in a yard that looked like no one had lived there for years. There were a few rubber tires laying on the ground, a couple of them half buried in sand. The yard was half sand and half weeds. The weeds had taken over, but it looked like at one time, someone had grown flowers in the tires. Next to one of the tired was a post suck in the ground with an old bird house nailed to the top. It looked as lonely and rugged as the trailer that sat next to it. We didn't go in right away. Gina just sat on the broken step. Quiet. It was here her tears really started to come out. I wasn't used to the crying 'cause where Gina and I lived, if you cried, you were weak. Our world kept us too busy for tears, and Gina and I, well, we were as tough as they came. We handled a lot of bullshit in our time, and we never really shed water over nothing. I guess it was different when it was the death of a real family member. This shit was real to her. I remember this 'causeit was here I really started to wonder and think about my family too. The real ones, that is.

After Gina finished her tears, we go in the trailer. It was pretty empty, with an old, rounded steel table sitting in the middle of the floor. There was an old chair with only three legs lying next to it on its side. There were a few cheesy wall hangings in the living room, but that's all that was in there. We made our way to the bedroom and found it just as empty as the rest of the place. Either Gina's sister was real poor, or some dumbass cleaned her out after she died. Gina didn't talk. In fact, she looked like a zombie as she made her way around the trailer, going from one room to the next. When she finally did talk, all she said was that she thought she could get at least ten grand for the place. Of course, she had to figure out how to sell it, and I was no help to her in that department either, so I told her to maybe make a sign that said, "For Sale."

There was really nothing to do at the trailer but to throw out the last of the stuff that was in there. Gina found some old papers in one of the kitchen drawers, but there was nothing helpful in them. There were no pictures of family, nothing that said Joan lived in the trailer. It was really sad. It really got me thinking of what kind of spread people would find on me when it was my time. Yeah, I got a few pictures of friends, but nothing that tells my story of being alive, picture-wise, that is. Anyways, Gina manages to find some cardboard and a pen and makes a sign that says, "Trailer for Sale, go see Maggie or Clint for details. $10,000." We leave the sign on the trailer in hopes that someone will buy it 'cause we really needed the money now to get home.

We walk back to Maggie and Clint's place, and Gina explains to them about the sign she made back at the trailer. She tells Maggie that if the trailer didn't sell in the next few days, that maybe Maggie can keep an eye on things. She told her that if she sold it, she'd share the profits with her. Anyways, Maggie and Gina finish talking about how to split the money when some guy in a suit comes knocking on Maggie's door. At first, me and Gina go sit in the living room 'cause we figure its none of our business until the guy asks for Gina Bishop. Gina gets up and goes to see the guy, and the guy is holding papers in his hand. He asks Gina if she is Joan's sister, and Gina tells him she is. The guy explains that he's a lawyer for Stockcliff and that Joan never paid land taxes for over ten years. He goes on to tell her that he was there to repo the trailer so that they can auction it off. Poor Gina—her face looked like she'd just seen a ghost. Ten grand, gone just like that. Me, well, I was worried about how we were going to get home with no money. I get up to go sit next to her, tell her everything is going be okay, and give her a hug. I knew my buddy was hurting real bad, and I had no idea how the hell to help her. We make a plan to go to the funeral home to pick up Joan's ashes so that Gina can have a quick send off for Joan in front of her friends. Maggie spent that day telling friends around the trailer park that they were having the service at her house that evening, so Gina says she will make good on that.

We manage to get to the funeral home right before it closed, and we retrieved Joan's ashes. The funeral people are kind and gave Gina a container for them. It wasn't the nicest container, but at least we weren't putting her in a paper bag. We get back to Maggie's trailer just as people arrived to give Joan a good send off. She didn't have a big pile of friends, but it sure seemed like the ones she had really loved her. Many of them were older, and I figured they grew up in the park with Joan and Gina. Gina knew all of them, so for her it was like a reunion. Gina and I made plans to leave the very next day with no money in our pockets and a container full of ashes.

We manage to get out of Stockcliff around five p.m. the next day, each carrying a backpack, some shopping bags, and the container with Joan's ashes. I am not sure why we waited for so long in the day to leave, but it seemed Gina was having a hard time letting go. Maybe it was more final for her this time 'cause she knew that for sure now she had no more family to come home to if she ever had to.

Our first ride got us as far as Dryden, and it was late when we got there. We hadn't thought about nighttime, but both of us were tired from the long day we had. We needed a place to sleep, and our ride dropped us off on the outskirts of Dryden, close to a graveyard. We walk for a bit, but Gina and me were real tired, so we decide to go sleep at the graveyard. We walk in, and Gina asks me if I'm scared. I tell her the way I see it, these people died somewhere else, so their ghosts are going to linger elsewhere. I tell her by the time the body gets to the graveyard, and if their ghosts or spirits (or whatever one wants to call them) are out searching for something, they ain't going to find it at the graveyard. Gina tells me that I make sense, so I tell her it wasn't ghosts I was scared of; it was people still living that could hurt us. Gina tells me she is less scared 'cause that really did make good sense. We keep walking and notice a shed on the other side of the graveyard. We decide to go see if the door is open and decide maybe we can sleep in there. The door is unlocked, so we open it only to find the shed full of junk, too much for us to squeeze in to sleep in, but we find a tarp in there so we pull it out. We make a bed with the tarp next to the shed, and it wasn't long before we fell asleep. We wake up the next morning to cops shaking us up. Sleeping in the graveyard cost us half a day of hitching, 'cause we had to explain why we were sleeping in a graveyard with a container of ashes at the cop station. The bugger couldn't just listen to our explanation where he found us and had to drive us into the station. I guess the good part of that was, he gave us a cup of coffee while we explained ourselves. Anyway, to make a long story short, our trip was more like fifteen days and not the seven days we had planned, plus I lost ten pounds on a count of not eating.

Anyway, I was lucky I didn't lose my job or my place, and me and Gina took a trip out of Vancouver a few weeks later to go pour out her sister's ashes in one of them beautiful flowing rivers. I still remember that day 'cause it really changed me and how I thought about stuff. Life, I mean. When we left that day, I didn't think that pouring some stranger's ashes in the river would do what it had done to me. It brought back some memories of being a kid. I mean, it was like when we would go to the lake when I was young. That flowing water just carried me to another place, and just like that, my mind started remembering things.

I remember when I was a kid, we lived in this area that had farm land, trees, a river, and a long lake. An image came into my head of me standing by the river with my mom and dad. I am not sure what we were doing there, but it sure got me lonely for Saskatchewan. As we were sitting there, Gina was crying, so I tried to comfort her by telling her that her sister is going home, back to the trees, the rocks, the water. And like always, I was making shit up to make her feel better. It kind of made sense to me that we all just go back to the ground and stuff, but I guess the way I talked made it sound like I was smart or something. It was beautiful thinking about it like that too. Gina just hugged, me and I told her that maybe it was time I go home too, back to Saskatchewan. I told her that I was going to save money for a few months, then maybe go back to Regina, 'cause that was the only place I really remembered well.

When Gina and I got back to Vancouver, I tell my boss my plans to leave. He tells me it's too bad 'cause I was the worker who stuck around longer than anyone else, and the first one who didn't steal from him. I tell him that I am glad he treated me well 'cause I know at times, I did do some things I wasn't proud of and maybe should have gotten fired for. In the end, he always gave me another chance, and I was happy about that. I didn't have too many who believed in me, so I knew I was going to miss him somewhat. He tells me he knows lot of people in Saskatchewan and if I needed help to call him.

I left a few months later, with a bag of clothes, some money, and a whole lot of memories of Vancouver. I left for Regina, saying it was not forever, but I felt that the least I should do was to go back to where part of my life started. I didn't have a set plan but figured that that Master Planner had a plan for me anyways. All I knew was that **I was looking for something to connect with**, I just wasn't sure what it was going to be. I knew I would know when I found it.

To spare all the boring in-between details, I didn't quite make it back to Regina but instead ended up in Elbow Summit just about forty-five minutes out of Regina. Elbow was a smaller city. It was the last place I thought I would end up. The ride to Saskatchewan, the not knowing what would happen to me—it scared me somewhat 'cause the first pay phone I saw in Regina, I used to call my old boss and tell him that maybe I do need one of his connections. He tells me to call him back in an hour and that he'd see what he can do. I call him back and he tells me he's got a cousin in Elbow Summit that could help me out if I could get there. I tell him I would make my way. So, I guess this is where my story starts with meeting the Evans family.

I read the story about me and Gina to Mr. Evans today. I make him a promise that one day I would leave and maybe go start looking for my brothers and sister. I wanted him to know that the longer I stayed with him and his wife, and the more I was learning to value family, the more I wanted one of my own. I just didn't want to leave yet 'cause I knew he needed me, or maybe I needed him too. I tell him that I'm not going to leave yet, and that I would be there for as long as he needed me to be. I wasn't really sure why I was telling him that, but maybe I needed to convince myself that he needed me more than I needed him. I knew deep down inside that this was not true because I came to really rely on this time with him. It seemed like I was finally coming together as a person, and it scared the shit out of me. I think this is what they call "growing up." I knew that I eventually wanted to go find my family, but I needed the courage and the strength, and the more I sat and thought about it, the closer I came to finally making that leap to leave. **I just wasn't there yet**.

I read to Mr. Evans every day, and each day I watch his face to see if there is life. Lately, those face movements I once noticed were not there as much. I will admit that something was off about him. Mr. Evans, well, it seems like his spirit to fight is gone. It's crazy, I know, but I spent so much time with him, and it seemed that I could sense these things. I somehow knew what type of mood he was in. He seemed so tired lately, and he just seemed different somehow.

A few days later, Mrs. Evans came home with red, puffy eyes. She tells me that the doctor had called her earlier that day to meet with her. Mrs. Evans goes on tell me that the doctor did some tests a few weeks ago, and they found cancer in Mr. Evans. Mrs. Evans, she starts to cry now, and I start to cry with her. It seemed like my heart broke into a million pieces that night. Mr. Evans was a good man, and to suffer this much was just not fair. I wanted to jump up and down and swear, but something in me stopped. I wanted to punch a wall, smash something, but even this part of me was gone. I really didn't know how I was feeling, but I figured it was the pain from sadness.

LOSING MR. EVANS

I haven't written for a few months; my mind has been somewhere else, mostly with Mr. Evans. The story about Me and Gina was the last one I shared with Mr. Evans. Mr. Evans passed away two and a half months after I told him that story. His body just shut down one day. I don't know if it was the cancer, or if he got tired of just being. I couldn't imagine what it was like for him. I wonder if he heard me read to him? I wonder if he heard his wife talking to him every day? My guess is, he did hear her, and maybe it was very painful to hear her voice, and there was nothing he could do about it. I wonder if he just got so tired of trying to wake up and couldn't. Can't say I blame him much. My guess is that he heard all we tell him. I know that in that sleeping body, there was a mind that was awake. At least, I want to think that.

The funeral for Mr. Evans was real big. Many people come out that day. It was sad 'cause none of them really came to visit him when he was at home in his coma. But maybe for them, he was kind of not there already. I guess this funeral just felt final for them. I don't know. I guess I am just trying to understand people differently. When I was out living to survive, people were just a part of my survival game. Never really had a whole lot of time to try to figure them out this way. I felt the loss too. It was crazy to think that my best friend in the end was a guy in a coma. When I think about it, he really was the only person that I could talk to, and I knew he wouldn't judge me on my crazy past. He didn't give his two cents 'cause in my time, I had enough assholes trying to give me advice I sure didn't want. I figured that I made it this far on my own and really didn't need others telling me what to do. I didn't drag any kids into my hell hole of a life, had no asshole husband beating on me, so I figure I done pretty good of taking care of Stella. I was tougher than some thought I was. Maybe I had no fancy education, but I was smart enough to know about life. Even at the funeral, I'd seen how some of them white folk look at me like I was some sort of leech. Maybe it did seem odd to see a brown woman living in these parts, but that was for us to live and not them. I know for the Evans, they were blind to the colour of skin, but sadly, a lot of them folks still seen my brown skin. Anyway, besides the sneering looks, the funeral was nice, and the house smelled real nice too with all the flowers and food that folks brought. In the end, it didn't matter to me what anyone thought, I had lived life not giving a shit about what others thought, and I was dammed if I was going to start caring now. I was only here for Mrs. Evans. She was all that mattered right now.

Mrs. Evans, she sure missed Mr. Evans. I could see it in her eyes. She slowed down so much that I worried about her. That is why I was glad she asked me to come live with her for a bit. I told her that I'd make a deal with her—that I will come live with her until she feels strong enough to be alone, then it will be time for me to go and find my family. I tell her not to rush on my account 'cause maybe there will be no one when I get to where I am trying to go. I tell her it's good for me too 'cause I need to save some money for my trip. She was happy with the deal. I figured that at least if she got tired of me, this was a nice way to get rid of me. I wasn't sure how this living arrangement would work for me 'cause I was used to always being alone, and being with Mr. Evans was kind of like being alone without really being alone.

Mrs. Evans didn't work as much, and she ended up hiring someone to help run the store. It was just as well 'cause it gave her time to teach me how to drive. That's right. You read me right. I was going to learn to drive. Anyways, how all that happened was, this one night, me and Mrs. Evans got a bit far into her wine collection. By the end of the night, I was the proud owner of Mr. Evans Ford Mustang, with the promise I would learn to drive. Booze got me into some bad situations, but nothing where I made promises like this. I wasn't sure I could keep my end of this bargain, but for the sake of the car, I was going to give it a try.

I missed Mr. Evans 'cause I got used to that time with him. I could think about what I'd done in my life, and I had time to think about the word "family." I liked how I could share my stories with someone who would not tell me how crazy I was. I liked that I could think about things I'd done but with no regret 'cause no one was around to ask me stupid questions or give me their two cents. I didn't need nobody's judgement on me either, so he was the perfect friend for me. Yeah, I done some crazy shit, but shit was shit. Life was life. I done it, lived it, and now it felt good to tell it. These last months were hard on me too, and I knew I had lost something special; I lost a way of living I got used to. Judy lost her husband, but it was like I lost the only ears that would listen to me. I guess it was like going to confession but not having to answer for my sins. I did my time just living in this crazy world, a world where they say there is a plan for us all.

I wonder what the big plans are for the kids that get killed in them wars on the other side of the world? I wonder what the plans are for the millions of poor people starving to death? I wonder what the plans were for the kids that were taken to them residential schools I read about? I sometimes wondered if my mom and dad had maybe gone to residential schools and maybe that was why they turned to the booze to forget. Pain does stuff to a person. Living the way I did, I seen how so many try to bury the pain through booze and drugs and other stuff. I get mad sometimes thinking about that stuff, so I try not to think too hard. In the end, I guess I'm only in charge of trying to think about the plan that was made for me, if there even is one. Imagine the life of the "Master Planner." How does one decide who will suffer and who will have it easy.? Maybe it's just best I don't think about this stuff and just go with the plan that was set for me. I guess I just see so much suffering on those with dark skin and wonder. That's all. But like I said, I can't dwell on that stuff and have to focus on the present.

My driving lessons with Judy didn't last too long before she went out and hired a professional to teach me. I got my learner's license in just four tries and now all I had left was the driving part. After getting my learner's, Judy took me around her block, and I damn near ran over a cat. I got them peddles mixed up and pressed the gas instead of the brake. Thank goodness that cat was fast. The cat was black too, so I guess the bad luck would have been on him. Mind you, I would have felt like shit if I hit him, and I sure was glad I didn't. Anyways, Judy tells me it's best get a professional, and so she hired one. It took a lot of courage for me to drive, but in just a month, I was driving around Elbow on Sunday afternoons like nobody's business. Judy and I made a deal that once I got my driver's license, it would be time for me to leave to go find my brothers and sister. This sounded good to me.

The next few months went by fast. I was practicing my driving skills, helping out at the store, and in the home. One night, Judy and I went into her storage house. Yeah, she had a storage house.

It wasn't a big house, but it was heated, and it had an old couch in there for us to sit. There were tubs of stuff. Stuff Mr. and Mrs. Evans had collected over the years. To me, it was just stuff, but to her, it was their life and memories. Each tub was like one of them time capsules. It told stories of their life together. As she opened each tub to look through, it made me sadder and sadder. I had no tub, no time capsule, nothing for anyone to open when I was gone. When I used to walk on beaches, I would look behind me and watch my footprints get washed away. Was this how it was going to be for me when I died? If there are tears shed, will they be like them waves that washed away my footprints? I tried not to think about things like this, but somehow watching friends lose loved ones showed me a different kind of pain. Judy was getting stronger, but I knew she would never be the same as she was when Mr. Evans was alive. I guess this was the same for me, I knew I wasn't the same person I was when I first got to this place. I know I wasn't looking for this life but was glad I had found it.

WHAT THAT SONG DOES

It was summer when I finally managed to get my driver's license. I had managed to stay with Judy for over a year, and she and I became close enough that if things didn't work out for me where I was going, she said I always had a place with her. This made me feel better about leaving, and I knew it really was time to leave. This trip didn't feel like the others. Long ago, I used to go, just go. Catch a bus, jump in with a buddy or thumb a ride—it didn't matter. Destination unknown. But that was the old me. Well, no, the younger me. The new me, or the older me, wants to know stuff now. I want to know who I am, who my family is, where I come from. I don't know. It all seems like something a person does before they is getting set to pass or something. It also felt kind of nice to have a home to come to if I didn't find my own. At least, it was a place. And I even got me a tub full of stuff to call my own. There isn't much in my tub, but it is a start to leaving a few footprints behind for those who want to see them.

Driving made me feel free. It felt pretty cool. It was nice. I didn't drive fast, but at least I could go where I wanted to go as long as I had money for gas and my car was working. Judy paid for my car registration for a year. It was kind of like a going-away gift. And as much as I like having a car, there is so much to look after. Shit, I struggled for years just to look after myself, let alone a car. But I guess it was better than a kid. Imagine that—me having a kid. The way my life was, my poor kid probably would have ended up in the same system I came from. I was lucky at some homes, but others were not so good. Over the years, I met many brown skins that came from foster care. Some good stories, but a lot of real bad ones too. I don't think I could live with myself if my kid ended up that way, so it was just as well that I had none. I sometimes sit and wonder too where my life would have gone had my parents not died. Would we have still been taken away and put into care on a count of them boozing and all? I know thinking about this stuff doesn't change anything, but still, I did have time to think and question. I knew the road home was going to be a long one, but I was stronger and more ready.

I loved having a car, and it was something I never dreamed I'd have. And I didn't just have any car; I had a Mustang. A car that many looked at when it drove by. But it must have looked stolen when a brown woman was driving 'cause it certainly didn't look like I could afford it. It even had one of them CD players in it. When I was working at the store, I met a girl who knew how to put music on them CDs, and when she found out I was leaving, she told me to give her a list of songs I want to listen to. She ttold me not to be shy about the songs 'cause she know how to find any song. I gave her a list as long as my arm. I put songs on there that I hadn't heard in years—songs that held stories.

I left early one morning with my windows rolled down and my first CD in the player. The first song that played was "Lyin' Eyes" by the Eagles. Man, I loved that song. I found myself singing,

"Birch Creek girls just seem to find out early, how to open doors with just a smile, rich old man she won't have to worry."

That song had story upon story. First person that comes into my head is good ol' Jack. Man, I hadn't thought of that guy in a long time. We loved this song. Sometimes, Jack would ask me a funny question like whether I would shack with an old man for his money. Then I'd laugh and ask if I had to put out. He'd say, "Yeah," and then I'd say, "Yeah," in a real dreamy voice. Then we would laugh together. I wonder if Jack and I would have made it. You know, to last long and stuff, had his stupid ass not got him into jail. I guess I could have waited, but time was never my thing. I was always on the move, like a coyote.

Another memory that song made me think about was that time I ended up in Yellowknife. Now, there's a story. Man, I haven't thought about this one in a long time. I was in Edmonton this one time, when I end up in a bar that had a live band playing. Now, you got to remember that I was a looker back then and could have easily found myself one of them sugar daddies that the Eagles is singing about in that song. Anyways, the band was playing, and I had no plans for nothing. Only plan that night was to find some poor suckers that would buy me drinks so I can drink my sorrows away. This much I remember. So anyways, the band, they take a break, and I go outside to have a smoke when one of the band members come out to smoke. He was the drummer, and he had quite the stick, if you know what I mean. Anyways, we get to talking, and we hit it off real good, and the next thing I know, him and I are kissing behind the bar the next break he has. Anyways, the band was leaving that night 'cause they have a gig in Yellowknife in a couple of days. I remember this 'cause Little Drummer Boy there, he asked me to go with him. But I'm drunk and stupid and I'm thinking he's the one, so I say, "Yeah, ok."

Well next thing you know, I'm in a van with the band. Man, when I think back to what could have happened. I was so stupid.

Anyway, we party and sleep most of the way. The band had two sober drivers, and they take turns driving all the way. I was drunk most of the way, so of course, I have no fricking idea where Yellowknife is. I remember falling asleep, waking up, drinking again, and going back to sleep. That's how far it was, but like I said, I had no clue. At one point, I am not sure where we were, but anyways, we all pass out, and next thing I know, we are parked outside a motel, and it's dark again. So, the guy I'm with, he gets a room for us, and well, I don't have to paint a picture of what happens next. But you know. We finally go back to sleep, and I'm sleeping real hard when all of a sudden someone is banging on the door. At first, I thought it was one of the other band players, but this guy I'm with starts freaking out and telling me to grab my clothes and go hide in the bathroom. I do what he tells me to do, and now I hear him opening the door and some woman is yelling at him. She's asking him who the fuck he has in the room with him, and he's telling her no one. She's yelling and asking him why the hell he didn't call when he got back, and he's trying to explain that they got back real late and that he didn't want to wake her up. Meanwhile, I'm freaking out in the bathroom, trying real hard to get my clothes back on when I realize that I forgot my panties in the room. I'm praying real hard the crazy woman don't find them, but the praying it don't do me no good, 'cause the next thing I remember is the door being pushed in, and the woman in the bathroom with me. Man, she was like one of them dogs that got distemper, and she just attacked me. Luckily, Little Drummer Boy grabs her from behind and pulls her off. I don't stick around and ask questions; I run out the door with all my clothes on except my panties.

I run to the next room where the other band members are staying, but no one is opening the door. I decide to try to figure out how to get back to Edmonton. I will get to how the song comes into this story soon. Anyways, there is this truck stop and café alongside the motel we are at, so I go into the café and ask if anyone is headed to Edmonton. If my luck would have it, a middle-aged man is sitting there eating when he waves at me to come sit with him, so I do. I tell him my story, and he says he's headed to Edmonton, and I can get a ride. I tell him I'll wait for him to finish eating and would wait outside, but he tells me to sit down and offers to buy me breakfast before we hit the road. Once we are done, I climb into his big rig and get ready for the ride back. Now, you have to remember that I was drunk when we came, so I have no idea how long the ride is. I am also with a strange guy for the ride, but somehow, he seemed trustworthy enough. I think I got the real trust when he started talking about his wife and told me that she was Native. That was the term he used. Anyways, he tells me she is from Hobbema. I felt safer with him than that psycho woman that was looking to bust me up. We get on the road, and he turns on his radio. The first song that plays is "Lyin' Eyes," and for some reason, that song made me think about that long, lonely ride back to Edmonton. To end this story, I did see Little Drummer Boy a few years later, playing at another rundown bar, and I really wanted to go ask him what he did with my panties. I laugh now at this story 'cause it is funny to think I rode commando all the way to Edmonton.

Another song I got on my CD is "Listen to the Music" by the Doobie Brothers. Now, that is a song I will never get bored of. This was the song for fast boys with fast cars. Maybe that was where I went wrong; maybe I should have looked for slow boys with fast cars, or better yet, slow boys with slow cars. But that song, yeah, it brought back some crazy memories. There was this guy I knew back in Chief Meetos' Reserve; they called him Hot Rod Harry. I haven't thought about Hot Rod in a long time. But anyways, this one time, there was this big party at a place they called "the Pit." That's what it was: a pit. A gravel pit. The Pit was about fifteen miles out from Chief Meetos', and in the summer, it was a popular party place. Hot Rod was a good friend of Donna's and showed up one nice summer evening, asking if us girls wanted to go with him to a pit party. Hot Rod had this beautiful black Trans Am. The kind Burt Reynolds drove in that movie, *Smokey and the Bandit*. Of course, we say yes and jumped into his car. The one song he played was "Listen to the Music" by the Doobie Brothers. As that song blared, Hot Rod punched the peddle and we flew down that road like bats out of hell. I still remember the rush. The feeling of freedom under the rubber tires and the roaring engine. Later that night, I got to hear another type of roaring engine. Crazy times. Anyways, we got to the party and there were about twenty cars parked all around. People all over. It was a crazy night, like many of the other pit parties. Most parties would end with fist fights, arm wrestling, and cars doing donuts in the open pit, spitting dirt at everyone. There was booze, pot, sex, and bonfires. The parties didn't died down until the sun came up and the last drop of liquor was gone. We were reckless. The smart ones would pass out in their cars until they slept it off, but the dummies would drive back, some drunk. Some of them parties ended real bad too. I tried my best to always stay put where I was partying 'cause I knew how some of those drives ended. Even lost a friend or two to a drunk driving accident. I was crazy, but I valued life a little bit.

Anyway, that particular night, Donna ditch us for some guy she met with a cheap perm and a red Cordoba. Yeah, his car was shiny, but that hair! All I could think about was him sitting in a chair with curlers all over his head. Something I did not find attractive. He had these fake ring curls, or ringlets—whatever the hell they were called— hanging down his back. Thought he looked sexy, but in the end, it was a fucking perm. Anyways, Donna liked Big Perm, or his car. I wasn't really sure, but she ended up taking off with him. Anyway, I wasn't too worried 'cause I knew I had a ride with Hot Rod. I figured we'd just end up sleeping in his car for the night 'cause he was drunk. One good thing about Hot Rod was he didn't drive when he had been drinking. I guess a few years back, Hot Rod lost his license for a year 'cause he was driving drunk, and he took out some guy's fence on the Rez. It was in the middle of the day, and I heard the worse part was that the guy was outside when all this went down, and he chased Hot Rod down with his truck. When Hot Rod's car finally came to a stop due to a flat tire, the guy dragged him out and beat him with part of his fence post. Hot Rod didn't charge the guy for the beating, saying the fence could have been the guy's kid, and he needed a good reminder never to drive drunk again. Hot Rod lost his licence for a year for that. I guess that was his lesson, so I knew we weren't leaving the pit that night. Anyways, I was getting pretty hammered and needed to sleep it off, so without really thinking about Hot Rod, I crawled into his car, rolled the window down a bit, locked the doors, and passed out. I figured Hot Rod had his keys, so he'd get in the car with them. Well, that didn't happen, and Hot Rod ends sleeping against the back tire of his car. The awful part was there was lots of mosquitos that night. I end up waking up to the sound and bites of the mosquitos, and a bladder full of beer. I jump out of the car and walk around the corner, almost tripping on Hot Rod, who is passed out near the back tire of his car. After I finish pissing, I walk up to see if he's ok. He's sleeping on his stomach, his face hidden in the folds of his arms. Anyway, I start to shake him, 'cause now I am thinking maybe he's dead, but after a few shakes, he finally turns over. Man, he looked like shit. Someone had taken a marker and drawn cocks all over his face. I wanted to laugh, but shit, he was my ride home, so I tell him to look at himself in the mirror. I give him fair warning of what he's about to see. He flips out when he sees his dick-covered face and punches his mirror right off the car. So, here I am, hungover as shit, hungry, and trying to calm this guy who is now bleeding from his hand. Anyways, I manage to find a jacket in the trunk of his car and wrap his hand. We look for some water or liquid of any kind but find nothing.Hot Rod says, "Fuck it, let's just go," and so we get into his car and drive off.

We get about halfway back to the Rez when suddenly the car comes to a rolling stop. Just our fucking luck! We ran out of gas. Hot Rod figures some asshole sucked out his gas with a hose while we were passed out. We decide to walk the rest of the way back to the Rez. As we are walking, I start laughing and telling Hot Rod we must look funny with his dick face and wrapped-up hand. Hot Rod, he laughs too and adds, "And your mosquito-bitten face."

These songs sure had a way of awaking these memories. They were a good way to pass the time and to refocus from what I was really feeling. Here I was driving back to the first place I ever called home, and I was scared shitless. I was never really scared of anything 'cause I never knew where it was going to take me. Now that I knew where I was going, I was scared. Maybe not scared of the place, but scared of not finding what I was looking for. I never expected anything from life, so anything I got was just what I got, and I could never complain 'cause I wasn't expecting it anyways. If that makes sense. So, here I was; I knew what I wanted to find but scared it wouldn't be waiting for me when I got there.

The drive "home" was nice, and my car had air conditioning too. I liked how the breeze felt when I drove with the window open, so mostly I drove with it down. I figured I was probably saving gas by not using the air conditioner anyways. I also drove slow 'cause I was really scared of getting into an accident, so I decided not to pass other cars. I finally got to the main road that led to Prince Albert, but it was going to be a long drive. There wasn't much to see on the drive, so my tunes help keep me focused. I never knew what it meant to really feel free until now. I mean, I was always free, but I never had a destination most times, and I was usually just riding the wave of life.

This time, freedom felt different. Kind of reminded me of that song by Queen, "I want to Break Free". It seemed as if I'd fallen in love for the first time—with life, and maybe this time it was for real. I can't really explain it. That feeling of wanting to know something or find something but being scared of knowing, or maybe scared of not finding it. This was how I was feeling. A part of me wanted to find my family, but I was scared of what would happen if I didn't find them. And yet, going to look for them felt like I was living for the first time. I think Mr. Evans would have been very proud of me right now. I wondered if my mom and dad were guiding me too.

As I was driving, another old, familiar song came on. Now this is a good story. Anyways, like I said before, I've been all over the countryside, met lots of people, had lots of laughs, and lots of crazy memories. I had this friend one time. Well, ok, I will admit it. There was once this guy I thought I fell in love with, and he and I were real close. I was already living in Vancouver, and he was living there too. He lived in the same neighborhood I did and worked at the bar serving drinks. His name was Eric, and he was this real sexy Aboriginal man. You know, the kind with sweet brown skin and hair that hangs down in the back. Man, I use to daydream about him as I watched him work. Pretend I was twisting his black hair in my fingers. Anyway, Eric really liked that song, "Come on Eileen," and when the bar was empty, he would throw some coins in the jukebox and play it over and over. One day, I got brave and asked him about his sex life and if he had one, and he tells me he's going through some things right now. I tell him that maybe after our shift we get a few drinks, and he can talk to me. He agrees, and all I'm thinking is he's on the rebound, and I was going to take the catch. Anyway, Eric comes over after our shift, and we sit down and share a case of beer and a game of cards. Eric is getting a bit drunk, and he starts talking about his personal life. He tells me that he's been going through some stuff and just needed someone to talk to. I tell him that I am there to listen as his friend. So, he starts telling me that he thinks he has a problem or something because he has weird fantasies about having sex in a graveyard. Now, I am a good friend and a good listener to those who want to talk, but I wasn't sure if I was in a position to give advice about things like this. But I try anyways. I tell Eric that maybe he should give it try. After all, he wasn't hurting anyone by doing the deed in a place where no one is living. I wasn't taught about respect and things like that, so to me, things are just as they are. Anyway, after that night, I don't see Eric again for a few weeks, and when he finally comes back in to work, he don't want to talk to me. After a few days, the silence is killing me, so I finally ask why he is giving me the cold shoulder. He tells me that he took me up on my advice on having sex in the graveyard, and as him and his date are doing the deed, they get caught and arrested. He tells me that he got thrown in jail for two weeks for it and was mad at me for telling him to do it. I could never understand people. Some want to be told what to do, then when they are told, they blame the world if things don't work out. I decided that Eric is not that sexy after all.

It took me six hours to get to Prince Albert, and I could feel my nerves running high. I was so close, and yet in my mind, **I was a million miles away from somewhere, maybe nowhere**. I hadn't been to these parts in so long, so I was surprised that there was some familiarity. I arrived in time to get a hotel room, and I was anxious to use the credit card Judy had me purchase to use. Here I was in my fifties, and I'd never had a credit card. There were many firsts for me that day, and I will admit it felt pretty damn good. I decided to stop at the first hotel I spotted, which was just off the highway. I knew tomorrow was going to be a long day, and I knew I needed my sleep.

THE LAST CHAPTER OR THE BEGINNING? BIRCH CREEK

I didn't get much sleep, and it seemed my stomach was doing flips all night long. At one point, I thought I would get up and go looking for a bar. That's what the old Coyote would do, but I really wasn't into that anymore. Maybe I did change—I don't know—but living with the Evans family and seeing how life can be without the booze or pot was kind of cool. Anyway, I pack up my bag and check out early that morning. I wanted to take my time driving to Birch Creek. I didn't have much sleep, and it seemed as if butterflies had moved into my gut. I go outside, and for a split second, I look towards the highway I had just driven on the day before, forgetting I had a car to get into. That part of my hitchhiking brain must have kicked in, and for a split second, I thought I was going to go hitch a ride. Man, that would have been funny if I forgot my car in the parking lot. I stop and giggle at myself for thinking about that and keep walking toward my car. I get into my car and sit in there for a long time. A part of me just wanted to turn around and head back south, but I knew I had to do what I came to do, and that was to find my family.

In my time, I had been to a few Rezzes, and sadly, I seen lots of things that I didn't want to see. I seen lots of drinking and stuff, and I guess a part of me was scared that maybe that's how my family was going to be. It had been, after all; it was booze that killed my mom and dad. I also felt ashamed for thinking these things. Shit, I was the oldest in my family, and I should have come back long ago to find my brothers and sister. But life just kind of snuck up on me, and next thing I know, I am older. I knew this drive was going to be a hard one, but I was here now, so I figured I would just keep going.

I pulled out of the parking lot and headed north. My first flashback came when I crossed over that big bridge leaving Prince Albert. I still remember crossing that bridge when they took us away from our home. I remember sitting in the back seat of that car that came to take us kids away, never to see each other again. I haven't seen that bridge since I was that little girl, and crossing it brought tears to my eyes. I hate crying, but sometimes when the water wants to leak, that damn stuff is just going to come out by itself. The bridge got me thinking about my mom and dad and how they crossed it one last time before the accident. I bet they thought they were just crossing it to come home, and sadly, they never made it. So, here I was, crossing that bridge again and hoping to get home too.

The turn to Birch Creek was another twenty minutes or so, but I decided to drive a bit slower. I had a map with me, and so I knew where I had to turn. I hadn't been here for a long, long time, so I wanted to take my time to look at all the things that had changed. Driving the first few miles seemed to take forever, and I was lucky there were two lanes. I am sure I would have caused a traffic jam. Just outside of PA was a group of stores, and I remember there was a gas station there. I remember my dad stopping there when I was a kid and gassing up sometimes. He would let me go in the store with him and I would buy candy. I decided to pull over and park in that same area where I thought the gas station was. I sat and let the memories come visit me, and it wasn't long before one did.

I must have been about seven years old, maybe younger, and my dad had told me he would take me to PA to go shopping for groceries. I don't remember why my mom didn't come, but I still remember it was just me and Dad. This was the time I figured out I was really scared of clowns. Anyways, I remember my dad pulling over to the gas station and giving me some change to go in and buy some candy. While I was inside, I guess dad started talking to a guy he met up with in the parking lot, and I think the guy gave my dad beer or something. Anyways, I don't think I was in the store too long when I come outside and see my dad sitting on the back end of this guy's truck, and they are just talking and drinking a beer. I recognized the bottle 'cause dad always had them laying around our place, inside and out. Anyways, I tell my dad to hurry up 'cause I want to go home, so he tells me he will just finish his beer, and we will get going. I am not sure what happened next, but this van pulls up next to the truck dad is sitting on, and the van door opens. One guy comes out and starts talking to the same guy dad is talking to. Funny how I remember this. Anyways, as they are talking, I'm sitting in the car with the window rolled down, parked next to the first guy's truck. I remember the van door opening, and a person comes out. What scared me was how they were dressed, and how their face was painted all up. Maybe this was my first time seeing a clown, I don't know, but I remember getting real scared. I remember calling to my dad and telling him I want to go NOW! The clown, well, he must have seen me scared 'cause now he's walking toward me. I try real hard to roll up the window, but I am not fast enough. He starts talking to me and asks if I am scared of clowns, then tells me not to be scared. Maybe it was the way he said it that freaked me all out, but I start screaming for my dad, at which point the clown starts laughing and taunting me more about being scared. My screaming was enough to get my dad to the vehicle, and he asks the clown what the hell he's doing scaring his little girl. I think the clown was drunk 'cause he starts arguing with my dad and tells my dad his kid is a chicken shit. Well, that was all it took to set my dad off, and he punches the clown right in the mouth. The clown goes down, and there is blood coming from his mouth. I look toward the ground and see a few teeth and a big red nose laying there next to him. My dad gets in the car, and we drive off. My dad is still mad when we are driving, and he's swearing that if anyone ever hurt his kids, he will kill them. I knew then that even though my dad drank like he did, he loved us through the booze. I remember getting home later and my mom wrapping my dad's hand. He had cut it up pretty good hitting that clown in the mouth.

I sat there in that parking lot remembering this. There was a small store where I had stopped, so I get out to go buy a pop to drink for the road, again it seemed like I was taking my time going. I knew that within an hour, I'd be back to where my life started, and I was pretty damn scared. Anyways, I buy my ginger ale, leave the parking lot, and head north. It was not too long before I get to the turn to head into Birch Creek First Nation, my home.

In less than an hour of driving, I find myself back on my Reserve, searching for whatever was left of me, if anything. There was a big store that stood overlooking a river where I'd make my last turn home, so I decide to stop and use their bathroom. I walk in and ask the guy working there if there is a bathroom I can use, and he points me to the back. Real funny thing was, he used his lips to do it, and I recognize the gesture. But he didn't really use his lips as much as he used his chin, but I thought it was funny just the same 'cause back in Vancouver there were always jokes about us brown skins using our lips to point with. I use the bathroom, but now I am feeling sick to my stomach. I sit in the bathroom for a while and slowly get up to wash my face with cold water. As I am washing, I look up into the mirror that is hanging on the wall, and it was in that instant that I wondered who I really am. It was scary standing there on my home Reserve, not knowing where the hell my life went and where it might have gone if my mom and dad didn't die so young. And for the first time in a long time, I start to cry. I sit back down on the toilet seat and let the tears fall. I am not sure how long I was in there, but it must have been a while. I stay there until there is a knock on the door and someone on the other side of the door asks, "Hey, lady, you okay in there?"

I tell him I am fine and would come out soon. I pull myself together and tell myself that everything would be okay. I walk out back into the store, and before I leave, I extend my hand out to the man working and say, "Hello, I am Stella Coyote."

Well, the man looked like he was about to either shit himself, or like he had seen a ghost. He stands there, frozen, and this time it's my turn to ask, "Are you ok?"

The man looks straight at me, and instead of returning my handshake, he grabs me and hugs me real tight. Now I am confused about what is happening, when he steps back and says, "Hello, I am Earl Coyote."

After all these years, I was finally home.

CPSIA information can be obtained
at www.ICGtesting.com
Printed in the USA
LVHW101958121022
730543LV00004B/275